Down with Love

Now a Major Motion Picture

from Twentieth Century Fox

Starring

Renée Zellweger and Ewan McGregor

Written by Eve Ahlert and Dennis Drake

Adapted by Barbara Novak

Celebrity Photographs by Douglas Kirkland

Down with Love

HarperEntertainment
An Imprint of HarperCollins*Publishers*

HarperCollins books may be purchased for educational, business,
or sales promotional use. For information please write: Special
Markets Department, HarperCollins Publishers Inc., 10 East 53rd
Street, New York, NY 10022.

FIRST EDITION

Designed by Chris Welch

Insert photographs by Douglas Kirkland

Library of Congress Cataloging-in-Publication Data has been
applied for.

ISBN 0-06-054162-8

03 04 05 06 07 WBC/RRD 10 9 8 7 6 5 4 3 2 1

Acknowledgments

A work of art—whether it's a book, a movie, or a great-looking outfit with perfect accessories—is often a collaborative effort. And so it has been with *Down with Love*. My undying love and gratitude—and a lifetime supply of chocolate—to the wonderful ensemble of people who helped my beautiful story come alive. I can never thank you enough.

To Eve Ahlert and Dennis Drake, screenwriters extraordinaire, whose brilliant writing brought the passion, chaos, and humor of my life to the big screen.

To Renée Zellweger and Ewan McGregor, for making Catch and me look so good on-screen. Save us a seat at the Academy Awards!

To Debbie Olshan, our bubbly, energetic liaison at Twentieth Century Fox, who became so adept at juggling, Ed Sullivan would have wanted to book her for his show!

To Jane Friedman, who once confided that she used me as a role model as she worked her way up from a Dictaphone typist to become president and CEO of a global publishing house. Now *she* is a role model for women in

v

publishing everywhere! I am so pleased and proud to have HarperCollins publish my book.

To Hope Innelli, Theodore Banner's "better half," for first suggesting that I write this book. Our cabin in the mountains is yours whenever you need to get away from your hectic city life. (The key is under the mat.)

To my dearest friend, Jeffery McGraw, Maurice's "little helper," for his brilliant editorial insight, outrageous humor, and endless support and encouragement. (And for the lovely green velvet box of chocolates!) You made it fun, J.! (Lunch is on me till 2003—then it's your turn!)

To Mark—for all he does.

And last but not least, to my gal Friday, Cathy East Dubowski, without whom this book could never have been written.

Editor's Note

Dear Reader:

You obviously bought this book because of the byline on the front cover. Everyone's clamoring to see what Barbara Novak will pen next. The original contract was for a tell-all book chronicling her meteoric rise in publishing—from our favorite author—a follow-up to her sensational international bestseller, *Down with Love* (now in its twentieth printing, thanks to you, her loyal fans).

But let me warn you, you'll find another author lurking between the sheets of this book. Could it be Catcher Block?

Confused? Stay with us, dear reader. It will all be clear in the end.

—Vikki Hiller
New York, 1964

Barbara

I t's hard to believe the story that takes place between the first line of this book and the last.

After all, it's not fiction. It's my life.

What happened was so fantastic, my editor optioned the book rights to a Hollywood studio so they could make a movie about my behind-the-scenes escapades.

Unbelievable? Maybe. But I was there. And now I've agreed to tell all.

Some time ago I wrote a book called *Down with Love*. I had my own reasons, which you'll discover later on in these pages.

After collecting dozens of rejection slips, I finally sold it to an editor named Vikki Hiller—that's right, a woman—who worked at Banner House Publishing.

We'd collaborated by phone and U.S. mail. But at last I was going to meet her in person. She'd invited me to New York City for the release of the book.

As I shoved my way through the crowds in Grand Central Station, I had a sudden twinge of uncertainty. I was one of eight million people trying to stand out in the crowd. Did I really think anybody would pay attention to me?

But I had come too far not to see this thing through.

The line at the taxi stand was impossible. I glanced at my watch. Darn! I was going to be late!

Then I spotted a cab pulling up to the curb across the street. Holding on to my hat, I broke away from the crowd, dashed across the street, and ran around to the passenger door.

Just then eight protesters piled out, very conservatively dressed, each carrying a placard that read DOWN WITH THE BOMB.

I'm not really in tune with members of the beatnik crowd, but today I smiled at each one. Because I, too, was "down with" something. I could be carrying my own little protest sign.

I hoped my book would attract more attention.

I slipped into the cab and gave the driver the address. We were there in minutes. I paid him and dashed into the shining skyscraper that was Banner House.

As I waited patiently for the elevator, other well-dressed men and women joined me until I was just one person in a den of people.

Ding! When the doors opened, everyone shoved on ahead of me. When they closed, I was the only one still left.

I was going to have to be a little more assertive.

I pressed the up button and stood ready and waiting to dash inside.

As the doors opened this time, I was hit by a huge cloud of billowing smoke. I staggered back. As I coughed, my gloved hand groped for the emergency fire alarm on the wall.

But another gloved hand stopped mine.

"Barbara? Barbara Novak?"

I waved away the smoke. "I think so."

"Thank goodness you're here!"

The voice was awfully familiar. Could it be—?

I opened my eyes, and as the haze lifted I saw a pretty brunette wearing the most adorable tailored suit and matching six-inch heels step off the elevator holding a cigarette.

"Vikki?" I asked, with a little cough.

"Vikki Hiller! Your editor! In the flesh!" She slipped her hand in mine and gave me a firm, but ladylike, handshake.

"It's so nice to finally meet you in person," I said.

"I was afraid you hit a storm on your way down from Maine."

"No, it was all smooth sailing until I pressed the button for the elevator," I explained. "This is the first time I've done the twist before ten A.M.!" I added with a chuckle. "Am I a mess?"

"A mess?" Vikki looked me up and down as I adjusted my hat. "My goodness! You're gorgeous!" She pulled me by the hand into the elevator and began drafting a mental list of the things we had to do during my stay.

"We'll set up a photo shoot for the book jacket. Don't worry, there's plenty of time. The book doesn't come out for a week." Then she gasped, suddenly panicked. "One week! Oh, my!" Without missing a beat, she schooled her features and calmed herself down. "Don't be nervous! Cigarette?"

The elevator flew us up dozens of floors in seconds, dropping us off at the Banner House reception area.

As Vikki led me toward her office, a woman of about thirty-five caught up to us. Keeping pace with our quick stride, she held out an ashtray for Vikki, who was still puffing away.

"Barbara," Vikki said, "this is my secretary, Gladys. Gladys, Barbara Novak."

"I know!" Gladys exclaimed, beaming. She shook my hand. "I'm glad to finally have a face to put with the voice."

Just then a rather dapper man in an ascot hurried over. He was carrying a poster board covered with brown paper. "Vick, I need you to sign off on this pronto." He smiled at me and added, "Maurice Johns, art director. Barbara Novak—your cover!"

With a flourish, he uncovered a poster-size original of a book jacket. MY book jacket!

I eyed what was behind that wrapping the way a little

girl peers into the biggest gift box on Christmas morning.

The title *Down with Love* was boldly printed on a hot-pink arrow that pointed downward.

"Oh, Maurice!" Barbara exclaimed. "I love it! You put this in Gimbel's window, and they'll be able to see it from Macy's!"

"*Down with Love!* Hear, hear!" Gladys cheered. "I only wish someone had written your book twenty years ago, before it was too late for me."

I smiled and patted her hand. She was one of the thousands of women I hoped to reach with my book. "It's never too late, Gladys," I assured her.

Vikki initialed the art board. "Great job, Maurice! Sorry if the guys in Reproduction have been riding your tail."

"I'm not!" Maurice replied, giggling playfully.

GONG! Before I could stop myself, my eyes popped open, my lips pursed, and my head retracted like a startled hen's.

Of course, I quickly tried to look normal—without *looking* like I was *trying* to look normal just because there was something going on that I was too much of an unsophisticated hick to witness without my mouth gaping open. I aimed for that vacant, not-really-paying-attention half smile the luncheon models at Lord & Taylor wear when they're showing you the latest fall clothes while you're gorging yourself on a Waldorf salad plate—an expression that works well in many of life's stickier social situations.

With my shoulders clenched and that natural look firmly frozen in place, I slowly rolled my eyes sideways to take a peek. I had never actually seen a homosexual up close before.

At least . . . not that I knew of.

Maurice looked pretty normal to me. He was quite cute, actually.

GONG! My eyes popped and my mouth flew open. Oh, my gosh! I'd only been in New York a few hours, and I was already ogling homosexual men!

Struggling to restore a normal vacant smile to my face, I watched Maurice wrap up my cover.

I shook my head. How could you tell something like that about a person? I didn't have a clue. I mean, Maurice reminded me of my sweet old uncle Gene, for goodness' sake. My mother's brother.

The interior decorator.

The one . . . *who never married*!

GONG! My eyes bulged open and I craned my neck as Maurice hurried away to his office. *You don't suppose . . . ?*

But there was no time to think about all that now—I'd have to sort it all out later. The intercom buzzed just as Vikki lit another cigarette—her third since I'd met her?—and Gladys answered it.

"They're ready for you in the lions' den," she told us.

I gulped, suddenly nervous. " 'Lions' den'?"

"Don't worry," Vikki said with a smooth smile as she led

me down the hall to a pair of closed eight-foot-tall polished oak doors marked CONFERENCE ROOM. "You'll be fine. Just take a deep breath," she advised as she savored one last drag of her cigarette.

As the oak doors seemed to open on their own, I felt for a moment like kicking off my high heels and making a mad dash for the elevator in my stocking feet. What was I doing here? Did I really think I could pull this off?

But then I reminded myself. I was a single girl with a mission.

"Gentlemen," Vikki announced like an emcee at the Miss America Pageant, "this is Miss Novak."

Six men, ranging in age from their twenties to their sixties, rose to their feet around the large mahogany conference table. I extended my hand as each one introduced himself.

"E.G."

"C.B."

"C.W."

"J.B."

"J.R."

"R.J."

"O.K.!" I said, somewhat overwhelmed.

"O.K. can't make it," said one of the men—I think it was E.G. "He's down with T.B."

"What a shame," I said sympathetically. "Is it serious?"

"No, they're just having breakfast," E.G. replied. "T.B.

is Theodore Banner. You know, the owner of Banner House. The fella publishing your little book. That's his portrait there."

I gazed up at a large oil painting of Theodore Banner, the Big Boss. He gazed back at me with a cold hard stare. I shivered as if he could see what color lingerie I was wearing.

"Take a good look," C.W. said unpleasantly. "*You'll* never see him in person."

"Forgive me if we kept you waiting, gentlemen," Vikki said briskly as she showed me where to sit, "but Barbara hit a storm on her way down from Maine."

"So," C.B. said, "you've come down from Maine, eh?"

"You remember, C.B.," said E.G. "Miss Novak is the farmer's-daughter librarian who spent the long cold New England winter writing her manuscript by the light of a lonely oil lamp."

J.B. winked, leered. "And how does a farmer's-daughter librarian with a lonely oil lamp come to find herself on Madison Avenue addressing the senior editors of Banner House?"

Tough audience, I thought, but I refused to be intimidated. I was a working girl, and I'd encountered my share of men in the workplace before.

"Good advice and good luck," I replied. "The good advice was all mine," I added with pride, "and it's all in the book. The good luck was finding a great editor like Vikki."

C.B. chuckled. "I'm afraid I'm at a loss here, ladies. I'm not sure I know what Miss Novak's book is about."

Most of the other men chuckled and shrugged as well.

I know you're tempted to bite a nail wondering what I did next.

Well, most women might have dissolved like a deflated soufflé at the patronizing look he gave me. He was such a horrible little man! And I must admit, I felt just the teensiest wobble in my confidence.

But then the little weasel adjusted his glasses as if he were quite bored, and crossed his leg. A flash of white caught my eye—a full three-inch gap between his dark sock and his pants-leg cuff.

That's all I needed. He was obviously the kind of man who couldn't keep his socks up.

Without a break in my Miss America smile, I lightly touched my fingertips to my white hat. It perched perfectly on my head, and thanks to a girl's best friend, my White Rain extrahold hairspray, not a curl was out of place. Nothing like a new outfit and a tried-and-true hairspray to make a girl feel confident.

It gave me the extra boost of courage I needed.

I turned to my editor. Vikki feigned her own chuckle, but I could tell she was annoyed by the men's attitude. And not entirely on my behalf.

"I've been reporting to you on this book's progress every week for nearly a year," she reminded them. I saw a muscle twitch in her cheek.

"It's the book about love, C.B.," said F.G.

At least one of them was paying attention.

"Oh, of course!" C.B. said dismissively. "A *love* story."

"The ladies *love* the *love* stories," C.W. said, with a "what can you expect?" shrug.

"My wife loves her stories on the TV in the afternoon," J.B. added.

J.R. snorted. "All those stories, you're lucky if they get dinner on the table!"

All the men chimed in with complaints about their wives. I could sense Vikki trembling, about to lose her cool. I reached out a gloved hand, but it was too late.

"It's not a 'story'!" Vikki cried with sudden force.

The room fell silent. Half the men looked at her as if they were thinking, *What is* her *problem?* And the other half looked at her as if they knew exactly what her problem was. They blamed it on her time of the month.

Vikki leaned forward on the conference table and declared earnestly, "Miss Novak's book is a serious work of nonfiction entitled—"

"Vikki, excuse me," C.B. interrupted. "It's right behind you, would you mind pouring me a cup of coffee?"

Vikki pursed her lips in irritation. But if there was one thing all we working women knew, it was when to pick our battles, so she got up from her seat and reached for the percolator.

"—a serious work of nonfiction entitled *Down with*

Love," she continued, then stopped and shook the cof-feepot. "This is empty."

"Well, if you're making a fresh pot," E.G. said, "I'll have a cup."

"Count me in," J.B. piped up.

"Likewise," C.W. said.

"Ditto," J.R. chimed in.

R.J. waved his hand. "None for me, Vikki . . ."

"Thanks, R.J.," Vikki said, hurrying to set out the cups.

". . . I'll have a Sanka," he clarified.

Vikki shot me a look, took a deep breath, unplugged the percolator, and began to make some fresh brew.

"As I was saying," she continued over her shoulder as she yanked the top off the percolator, "the central thesis of Miss Novak's book, *Down with Love,* a serious work of non-fiction, is that women will never be happy until they are self-fulfilled. And women will never be self-fulfilled until they attain equality . . ."

She carefully removed the basket of used grounds. ". . . and become independent as individuals by achiev-ing equal participation in the workforce." She tapped the grounds into the trash, then quickly laid the basket on the counter and shook her fingers. "Oooh! That burns!" she muttered.

"And how do you propose women do that, Miss Novak?" C.B. asked as he waited to be served.

I grinned. That was my cue. Cool as a cucumber, I took over the meeting. "By saying 'Down with love'!" I proclaimed. "Love is a distraction."

Well, you would have thought I'd said, "I'm taking off all my clothes!" by the way the men stared at me.

There was stunned silence, and then everyone spoke at once.

"But if women were to stop falling in love, it would mean the end of the human race!" C.W. said in outrage.

"Not at all," I explained calmly, as if talking to a little boy. "I said women should refrain from *love*, C.W. Not *sex*."

C.W. looked puzzled. "Isn't that the same thing?"

The other men stared at him as if he'd lost his mind.

"I mean, for women," he quickly corrected.

Reassured of their comrade's sanity, the other men turned their attention back to me, a look of skepticism on their faces.

"It won't be," I explained, "after they've mastered the three levels outlined in my book that will teach any woman to live life the way a man does."

C.W. scoffed. "I never heard of such a thing."

Behind me, Vikki—struggling to open a new can of Chase & Sanborn coffee—said, "Yes, you have. Verbatim. That's the copy for the book jacket. I read it to you last week."

"Perhaps Miss Novak could elaborate," E.G. suggested.

"Certainly, E.G.," I said. "Level One instructs women to abstain from men altogether so they'll stop thinking that the pleasures experienced during the sex act are related to love. They are not—as women will learn by practicing the self-pleasuring technique I've detailed in chapter seven—"

The male editors leaned in, practically drooling on the conference table.

"—entitled 'Up with Chocolate.'"

"Chocolate?" J.B. said, mystified. "Up what?"

"You see, gentlemen," I explained, "the female has a biological reaction to chocolate that triggers the same pleasurable response in the brain as those triggered during sex. By substituting chocolate for sex, the female will soon learn the difference between sex and love. Love for a man will no longer occupy her mind.

"And since the woman will not be devoting her time and energy to making herself attractive to the chocolate, or making a home for the chocolate, or making herself seem interested when the chocolate tells her how its day went, she will find she has the time and energy to move on to Level Two, where taking on new challenges will lead her to the self-sufficiency of Level Three, where the woman becomes active in the workforce, earning and achieving an unequivocal equality with men."

"Who takes cream?" Vikki called out as she lined up eight cups and saucers for coffee.

J.B. looked like Rodin's *Thinker* as he tried to puzzle out this startling new concept. "And all this time the woman is abstaining from sex?"

I laughed. "Heavens, no! By Level Three she can have sex whenever she likes—without love—and enjoy it the way a man does—à la carte." I leaned forward. "She may even find she'll be able to give up *chocolate*."

"Are you *sure* this isn't fiction?" C.B. asked.

All the men chuckled. They resembled nothing more at that moment than a pack of hyenas, emulating one another's mindless barks.

But it was no less than I'd expected. They were men, lest we forget.

"I'm living proof," I argued. "After all, I'm the farmer's-daughter librarian from New England who finds herself on Madison Avenue addressing the senior editors of Banner House." I winked at the man on my left. "Isn't that right, J.B.?"

The men sat back, silenced. What could they say? I'd bested them, simply by standing there before them.

But E.G. leaned back in his chair with a smug condescending smile. "Well, Miss Novak, your theories may have worked with the gentlemen up in Maine, but I'd feel remiss if I didn't give you a little fatherly advice. The men in Manhattan are not the fine, upstanding, straightforward men of Maine. The men of Manhattan are devious.

They're dangerous. They'll be coming at you from every angle."

Suddenly E.G. slid toward me in his chair. "When you're watching your front, they'll attack from the rear."

Another man slid up behind me.

I whipped around to face him.

"And when you're protecting your rear," E.G. hissed, "they'll drop out of the sky."

After that, the meeting roared out of control like some boardroom fraternity party. The jokes and catcalls and laughter didn't even die down when Vikki and I ran around the table serving them their coffee.

It was difficult, I must admit. I'd been prepared for some skepticism, but not this. I'd hoped for a warmer reception from the staff of my own publisher! But what did I expect? They were men, after all. And men relished their position on top.

The dogs!

But they all had wives. And secretaries. And mothers and sisters and maids.

Just wait till I get my book in their hot little hands and tell them:

We don't have to take it lying down!

CATCHER

We interrupt this book to tell you *my* side of the story.

I mean, after all, who's the one with the great big Pulitzer?

Besides, Barbara Novak might never have written this book if it hadn't been for me.

So let me start from the beginning, the first day I ever laid eyes on the *Down with Love* dame.

I was late for work, so my friends at NASA gave me a lift. Nothing but the best from the National Aeronautics and Space Administration. Take their aircraft of choice for short-distance flights—the Sikorski 500 Turbosomething. As helicopters go, it was fast, reliable, and comfortable. The one I was traveling in had a five-star general behind the joystick as well. Everything the modern air traveler could possibly want, in other words. Except the stewardess, of course.

Not that I didn't have plenty of company with me on my flight back from Cape Canaveral. The Bossa Nova

Triplets were along, dressed in sequin-spangled floor-show gowns from the NASA luau the night before. Rio, the most well rounded one, leaned over to blow me a kiss as I climbed down the chopper's exit ladder.

"Easy, baby," I said, eyeing the strain on her gown. "Careful you don't fall out."

From the last rung of the ladder I dropped to the roof and saluted the pilot, still wearing last night's party hat.

By the time I entered *KNOW Magazine*'s main lobby, my arrival was front-page news. The boss was already waiting for me. Only instead of "welcome back," Peter MacMannus said . . .

"You're fired."

Same old Peter, I thought, going around him. "No, I'm not," I said as I sat down in my office and took off my shoes.

Peter stomped in and stood over me like a prissy schoolteacher fussing at a kid who'd shown up late for school for the fifth time in a week. "Oh, yes, you are," he insisted. "So take your Pulitzer, and your beloved Underwood, and your change of underwear, and clear out!" He pointed a rolled-up newspaper at the door, as if I needed directions. Fortunately, there was a girl in the way.

"Do you work for me?" I asked, hoping the answer was yes.

She nodded shyly. "I'm Sally. I'm new."

"They're always new," Peter muttered, shutting the door, turning his undivided attention on me.

"You had a story due yesterday! But I gave you more time—I held the presses for you so you could get your scoop on Nazis hiding in Argentina. Then I see this." He pushed a pair of reading glasses onto his nose and read from the newspaper. "Item: *KNOW Magazine*'s star journalist, Catcher Block, ladies' man, man's man, man-about-town, was seen leaving the Copa last night with a doggie bag and three girls from the floor show!"

Oh, that. "I took the Bossa Nova Triplets to Cocoa Beach," I explained. "NASA was throwing a luau." Figuring that was enough, I stepped into the office's private bathroom and turned on the shower.

Peter wasn't through with me. His angry face appeared in the mirror over the sink. "Well, I hope you enjoyed it," he hissed, "because unless you found Nazis hiding at your luau, you're fired!"

I flashed him a smile and then stepped into the shower. My look was sufficient. I didn't have to draw Peter a picture.

"There *were* Nazis hiding at your luau!" he cheered. "I *knew* you'd do it!" Then he wiped a porthole in the shower door and pleaded for more. "What have you got for me, Catch? What have you got?"

"Argentina isn't the only hiding place for Nazis," I told him. There was a fresh bar of deodorant soap in the dish.

It smelled minty fresh, I was glad I used it, and didn't I wish everybody did. "They're hiding in Florida, too."

Peter was ecstatic. "Wow! How?! Who's hiding them?"

"We are," I told him.

"We? Americans? Why? Nazis are bad. We're good."

I let him mull it over in the leather side chair outside the bathroom door while I rinsed off. Then I grabbed a towel and wrapped it around my waist. Peter was waiting patiently for the rest of the story.

"Some bad Nazis are good scientists," I explained. "Like the genius who's building the rocket that will land us on the moon first and win the Space Race. He's a Nazi. And I saw the top secret file to prove it. Here. I brought you a souvenir."

I unclipped a NASA security-clearance badge from inside my dinner jacket, which was hanging on the bath-room door, and fastened it onto Peter's shirt pocket.

"Whoa!" he gasped, looking down and sinking further into his chair. "But how could you possibly see a top secret file?"

I grinned. "Blame it on the bossa nova!" I said, dancing cha-cha steps across the room.

"The Triplets?" Peter guessed.

"Yep! See, Lola shakes her maracas, and Rosa bounces her bongos, while Nena is all hands—a hundred and twenty words a minute."

I opened my briefcase and removed its contents, which

I handed over to Peter—a thick and neatly typewritten manuscript.

"The story?! It's written?! Wow, Catch! Is it safe to print? I mean, NASA is going to blow its stack!"

I went back to the bathroom and shook up a can of electric-shave cream. "They forgave Germany," I pointed out, spreading foam over my beard. "They can forgive us."

Peter pushed the talk button on my intercom and barked at Sally on the other end. "Get someone from legal up here." The gadget clicked and crackled a few times as the poor girl struggled with the new machine. Three times she tried to respond through the static, each time sounding farther and farther lost at sea. Finally she gave up and yelled through the door.

"Yes, sir!"

Satisfied, Peter opened a file drawer and fetched me a clean shirt, boxers, and socks. "Sorry I lost my cool," he said. "About your Pulitzer and your Underwood and your underwear, I mean. My analyst says I only react to you with such vehement loathing because I admire you so much. He says I resent you for being a self-made man, as opposed to being the son of a self-made man, as I am." Finished with his speech, he handed over the clothes. "I hope you have your garters from last night," he said. "There's none in there."

"Garters?" I had to laugh. "I haven't worn garters since Nixon conceded."

Peter's eyebrows went up. "What, are you turning into some kind of beatnik?"

I shook my head. "Step into the future, Mac. Garters are a thing of the past."

Peter hiked up his pants leg and studied his own gartered leg. "I don't know, Catch. I have enough of an insecurity complex without worrying about my socks falling down. How can you be confident you won't show a shiny shin when you cross your legs?"

I came out of the bathroom sans pants, giving Peter a good look at my socks. They were as snug as a second pair of skin, all the way up to just below the knee. "It's a miracle of the Space Age," I explained. "Sock manufacturers are using new wonder fibers like Lycra, Orlon, and Dacron to put super-stay-up power in their over-the-calf sock."

Peter was impressed. "Over-the-calf?"

I nodded. "It's the only way to fly. Sure, they make a wonder-fiber garter-length midcalf, but the longer length is the ultimate guard against a gauche gap between your hose and your trouser cuff."

The intercom crackled again, Sally struggling to learn it. The "talk" light was glowing at my end—she could hear us, at least.

"What would you say is the average length for most men?" Peter asked me.

I stepped over to the desk in case Sally tried to call.

"How would I know?" I said. "You think I stand around in the locker room at the club making a comparative study?"

Peter came over for a closer look. "Let me see yours again. We can measure. I'll get a ruler."

I sidled up to the desk, resting my leg across it. He fumbled around in the center drawer. "Better make it a yardstick," I joked.

The intercom light told me Sally was still there.

Peter came up with a twenty-four-inch metal ruler and laid it on the desk next to my shin. "Okay, now," he said, "let's be accurate. Make sure you've got it fully extended and you've got it up the whole way." I pulled the sock tight and Peter lined up the zero end of the ruler with the bottom of my heel.

"It stays fully extended the whole way all day long," I said. "That's the miracle I told you about. 'Better living through chemistry.'"

"So, what have you got?"

I put my finger on the ruler where the sock stopped over my calf. "Sixteen inches."

"Sixteen inches?!" Peter gasped. "How long does a man's hose have to be?" I glanced at the intercom. The light was still on.

"That's thirty-two inches of confidence in every step, Mac. Don't forget, I've got two of them!"

Something crashed in the next room. Peter and I rushed to the door together, and there, behind the desk, Sally had fallen over in her chair, out colder than the war with the Russians.

"I don't believe it!" Peter said. "You went through another one. That's three this month."

"What is it about the workplace that women just can't seem to handle?" I wondered aloud.

Barbara

Men!"

Vikki and I were in the backseat of a taxi riding across town. Thousands of people walked by in their hats and coats and carrying briefcases. Fabulous views of the world's most famous sites passed my window like picture postcards of New York City, but I didn't see any of them.

Upset? You're darn right I was upset. Believe me, it was a definite test of my twenty-four-hour roll-on.

"They want us to fail!" I fumed. "The nerve! Inviting me to New York to launch my book when they have no intention of promoting it."

Beside me, Vikki just smiled like a cat and patted my white-gloved hand. "Don't worry," she assured me, sounding awfully cocky for a girl in her position. "I have a plan."

That perked me up. "You do?"

She nodded and smoothed her already smooth dark do. "Remember last winter when you called me and said you'd like publicity where men would see it, too? Perhaps in a *men's* magazine, you said. A prestigious men's magazine?"

she added, hinting. "The most widely circulated and most highly respected men's magazine?"

"*KNOW?*" I gasped.

Vikki looked slightly annoyed. "Yes, you did."

"No—I mean <u>KNOW</u>. *KNOW Magazine: for Men in the Know.*"

She frowned, trying to follow. "Oh." Then her eyes lit up. "Yes! Exactly!"

I was so excited, I was nearly bouncing in my seat. "You got us advertising in *KNOW*?!"

"No . . ."

"Right!"

"No. I mean, *no*, I did not."

"Oh."

"I did better!" she exclaimed. "I've gotten you a cover story written by *KNOW Magazine*'s star journalist, Catcher Block!"

My heart nearly stopped beating. The name took my breath away. "Catcher Block?!" I was able to say at last. "The ladies' man, man's man, man-about-town?!"

Vikki grinned, and I thanked my lucky stars that fate had thrown my book onto this editor's desk. What a gal!

She had no idea what her announcement meant to me.

I threw my arms around her and squeezed. "Oh, Vikki! You're the best friend a girl from Maine who wrote a book and came to New York could ever have!"

"You don't know the half of it!" Vikki replied. "I hear that Catcher Block is gorgeous! And eligible!"

I frowned.

And Vikki winced at my expression of disapproval. "Uh, not that that matters to us." She sat up and pounded her knee with her fist. "Down with love!"

If she only knew what I was thinking.

I sank back against the seat and sighed. "I can't believe it. Me . . . on the cover of *KNOW*!

"*KNOW!*"

CATCHER

No!"

Peter and I were hurtling down Third Avenue in a taxi, a disorienting roller-coaster-like ride in a confined space that he was trying to twist to his advantage. His goal in life at the moment was to get me to do a cover story on Barbara Novak. In direct contrast to his wishes, I was trying to maintain my integrity as a professional journalist, ladies' man, man's man, and man-about-town.

"Catch—please?" he begged, looking especially pitiful because he'd lost his glasses again. "I promised! It's one cover story. A girl's never called me in my life, let alone invited me for a drink! I think this Vikki really likes me, and I think I might really like her. In fact, I'm sure I would if she really likes me. And she does, because I led her to believe that as the owner of *KNOW Magazine*, I had some pull with my staff!"

"Well, go pull your staff with one of your other writers," I told him, "because I'm not doing it."

"No. It can't be anyone else!" Peter said sulkily. "The

best thing I have to offer a woman is the same as the best thing you have to offer a woman: you!"

I understood his problem completely. "But I'm all tied up, Mac," I told him. "I'm using me."

Still, there was no stopping him. Years of pampering and privilege had developed in Peter a kind of dual personality—half pussycat, half German shepherd. Using his position as the owner of a major magazine to get a date didn't seem the least bit unusual for him. "Come on!" he pleaded. "It'll be fun! You like fun!" he added.

The driver made a hard right, throwing us across the bench seat. "Fun? Interviewing a man-hating, embittered, New England–spinster librarian?"

Peter frowned. "How do you know what she's like?"

Wasn't it obvious? "Who else would write a book called *Down with Love*?" I asked him. "I mean, you don't have to be a Nazi rocket scientist to figure that out."

Before he could answer, the car jerked to a halt in front of the Mahogany Room. I leaped out and left Peter to pay the driver.

Barbara

Beautiful, Barbara . . . just beautiful . . ." Vikki effused.

Flash!

I couldn't believe it. *Pinch me, I'm dreaming!* I wanted to shout.

Vikki had rushed me to the studio of a top New York photographer, and now this handsome thirty-something man named Anastagio Fabrizio was taking dozens of photographs of *me*—as if I were Elizabeth Taylor or Doris Day, instead of your average American girl. A girl who always needed Pepto-Bismol to make it through school-picture day.

"Let's try one looking over your shoulder," Vikki suggested.

I was warmed up and in the mood. I turned my back on Anastagio, then playfully gazed over my shoulder, and shot him a look from Chapter Twelve—as if he were some handsome stalker and I wanted to be caught. "How's this?"

"Beautiful, Barbara," Anastagio murmured, clicking away, "just beautiful."

I got the distinct impression that he might be admiring more than the drape and cut of my figure-hugging embroidered pink wool suit.

Flash!

Well, dear reader, I'm here to report that being photographed by Anastagio Fabrizio does oodles for a girl's morale.

Pinch me, I thought, *but please don't wake me up!*

I never dreamed literary endeavors could be so stimulating.

CATCHER

As soon as we entered the Mahogany, Henri—the maître d' and an old friend of mine—rushed to seat me at *KNOW Magazine*'s regular booth in the snazzy hotel's bar.

Peter followed me in, sat down hard, slipped on a pair of prescription Italian sunglasses, and buried his face in the menu, pouting. It had nothing to do with paying the taxi fare.

Louis, the headwaiter, arrived and demonstrated the art of fine table waiting by feigning a look of respect for Peter as a fellow adult. In truth, he knew my boss only too well. He'd been serving the man at the Mahogany since Peter was just a little associate publisher on his daddy's knee.

Peter stayed buried in the menu.

With a wink from me, Louis melted away to get us our usual aperitif.

"Lose your glasses again, Mastroianni?" I teased my boss. Peter had dozens of pairs, yet never seemed to know where any of them were.

Peter grumbled, still on the same jag. "Best friend won't do you a favor, I don't know who will."

Aw, jeez. Peter was turning on the guilt—a highly refined skill he'd learned at his *mother's* knee. "Do you know what you want to order?" I asked, trying to cut him off.

"All I know is if I were a ladies' man, man's man, man-about-town, and my best friend asked me to help get a date with the one and only girl who had ever shown an iota of interest—"

I'd avoided him at the office, and I'd dodged him in the cab, but now he finally had me, trapped at the table in the Mahogany like some hapless *KNOW Magazine* advertising client. Even though I could see right through his strategy, it was going to work. He was just too pitiful. Eventually I was going to give in. I decided to stop the suffering now.

His, that is. I had a feeling mine was just about to begin.

"Waiter?" I called, snapping my fingers. "Bring me the phone." Then I scowled at Peter. "You have the spinster's number?"

Ecstatic, Peter dug a card from his wallet, and then hovered like a schoolgirl while I dialed the phone.

Barbara

When you're a writer, sitting home alone in your cramped little office—pouring your heart and soul into your work, agonizing over every word, indulging in chocolate, too much caffeine, and the occasional cigarette to clear the air—you're far too consumed by your struggles even to dare dream of what comes after your book is finally published.

Well, maybe you do fantasize a teensy bit, but if you daydream too much, dear reader, you'll never get the thing written. That's one of the most important things I learned in secretarial school: to keep my derriere in my chair. That's the only way you'll ever finish typing that stack of business letters and reports the boss needs by five o'clock. And it's the only way you'll ever see your name on the cover of a book.

But when you do finish, one nice little fringe benefit is the perks. At least, if Banner House publishes your book. And if Vikki Hiller is your editor.

To make me feel at home, Vikki had rented me a snug

little New York City apartment so I wouldn't have to put up with hotels. As she led me down the hallway, I admired the decor. It was far more charming than any place I'd ever lived before.

Vikki jiggled the key in the lock and then opened the door. "I hope you won't be disappointed," she said as we stepped inside.

A small entryway led into a huge magnificent sunken living room. Plush white wall-to-wall carpet. Twenty-foot ceilings. A white marble walk-through fireplace between the living room and library. A very chic spiral staircase led to the upstairs bedroom. The decor was exquisite, the latest thing.

Grinning, Vikki crossed to the closed floor-to-ceiling curtains and pushed a button.

The drapery parted like the curtains in a theater, revealing a wall of windows that stretched the length of the apartment.

I gasped. I could see all of Manhattan below Sixty-second Street: the Fifty-ninth Street Bridge, the Chrysler Building, the Empire State Building, even—in the distance—the Statue of Liberty.

"Oh, Vikki," I squealed, "it's adorable!"

The phone rang again. I looked around.

A pink Princess phone! I'd always wanted one of those!

"My first New York phone call!"

Vikki gasped. "It must be *KNOW Magazine*! No one

else has your number." Her hand flew to her mouth. "It must be Catcher Block!"

We squealed like schoolgirls expecting an invitation to the prom.

Then quickly, before it stopped ringing, I calmed myself down and reached for the phone. "This is Barbara Novak," I said in a calm elegant voice.

"This is Catcher Block."

The man's deep, rich masculine voice nearly curled my toes. But no self-respecting girl would let a man like him know.

"Catcher Block?" I repeated, as if I'd never heard the name before. "Catcher Block . . . ?"

"*KNOW Magazine.*"

"Oh, yes." I counted to three. "What can I do for you, Mr. Block?"

The man had the audacity to laugh. "I think it's what *I* can do for *you*, Miss Novak."

I waited politely—and tried not to look at Vikki, who was literally hopping up and down in her high heels.

"I'd like to invite you to lunch," Catcher said, "so we could discuss your book."

"That sounds very nice," I replied politely, as if I'd gotten a hundred similar calls since breakfast, "but I'll have to check my schedule to see when I'm available."

"Well, we've already ordered," he replied. "Can you be in the Mahogany Room in ten minutes?"

Ten minutes!? The arrogance of the man! *Well,* I told myself, *you'd better let him know right off the bat who's calling the shots on this one.*

"I'm afraid that would be impossible, Mr. Block." I hoped my voice was suitably appalled.

I could almost hear him shrug over the phone line. "Some other time, then—"

"Right," I interrupted. "I'll be there in fifteen." And I hung up.

As long as I was calling the shots, I decided I might as well do what I was dying to do—which was to dash down to see him immediately.

Calmly I turned to Vikki. We looked each other in the eye. Then we squealed at the top of our lungs.

I got the date I'd been hoping for. No prom queen had ever felt more elated.

CATCHER

Peter removed his sunglasses and beamed. "Catch, you're the best friend a guy with twenty diagnosed neuroses could ever have!" he assured me.

"Well, we've been friends a long time," I said. "I knew you when you only had twelve."

Peter was practically beside himself with joy. He stood up to check the fit of his necktie in a mirror across the room, craning and dodging around so he could see himself past the wait staff and other diners milling about. "Oh, this is great!" he said, on tiptoe. "I'll be right back. I've got to put in my shoe lifts." He made a mad dash for the men's room.

Peter's timing couldn't have been better. No sooner had he left the table than a woman slipped up from behind me and held her hands over my eyes, as if we were playing blindman's buff. "Guess who!" she said. The accent was British. London area, but not downtown. She'd grown up somewhere in the small towns just to the north. Other than that, I had no earthly idea who she was. Her perfume was familiar, but it was a popular brand—I'd bought it for at least a dozen women myself. Let that be a lesson, guys. Different brands for different broads.

So I'd have to fake it. Chat her up a bit for a few more clues.

"As if I'd have to guess," I murmured.

"Tell me my *name*," she insisted. *That game.*

"Tell me you love me," I replied smoothly.

"Blimey, Catch! You know I love you!" she confessed.

It was now or never—she had a name, and it was up to me to remember it. "And I love you, too—" I promised, stalling, when suddenly it came to me. "Gwendolyn!"

She squealed in delight, and I pulled her into the booth for a serious greeting.

After a few moments, I wiped the lipstick off with my pocket handkerchief and asked, "How long is your layover?"

"Never long enough," she cooed playfully.

"There's always time for a matinee," I said with a devilish grin.

I escorted her out of the bar, leaving Peter to pick up the tab.

Barbara

*L*unch at the Mahogany Room. It was the kind of business meeting I'd only dreamed of before.

We told the maître d' we were expected, and he immediately showed us to one of the best tables in the place. At the moment the booth was empty, with two cocktail glasses perspiring on the white tablecloth.

The maître d' fawned over us a bit, arranging our table settings, adjusting the flowers. It felt wonderful to be fussed over, just for lunch.

Suddenly a nice-looking, well-dressed man with blond hair rushed over to our table, glancing around the restaurant with a worried look on his face.

Obviously not Catcher Block.

"Oh, hello, Peter," Vikki said pleasantly. "Barbara Novak. Peter MacMannus."

I extended my hand. "Nice to meet you, Mr. MacMannus."

Vikki looked behind him, around the restaurant, then back at MacMannus. "Where's Mr. Block?"

"Yes, Mr. MacMannus," I repeated, "where is Mr. Block?"

He opened his mouth as if hoping Catcher might appear by magic, and then simply said, "I don't know." He fiddled with the saltshaker, rearranged the flowers, and then spoke to the maître d'. "Henri, where is Mr. Block?"

The maître d' clicked his heels and bowed slightly. "I don't know."

"What kind of maître d' are you?" Mr. MacMannus exclaimed, his voice cracking.

Just then a waiter in a red jacket brought a courtesy phone to our table and announced, "Mr. Block for you, Mr. MacMannus."

"Ah! Here he is now!" MacMannus snatched up the receiver, and struggled to maintain his composure as he spoke into the phone. "Catcher, where are you? . . . Yes, she is." With a slight frown, he handed the phone to me. "Mr. Block would like to speak with you."

I took the phone. "This is Barbara Novak."

"Miss Novak," Catcher Block said. "I'm so sorry, the darnedest thing. I was waiting for you in the bar when a little English foxhound walked right in and came up to me and started nuzzling me. Well, she seemed so lost, and she didn't want to go with anyone else, I just had to take care of her."

"Mr. Block, that is so thoughtful," I said. "I remember reading that the true test of a man's character is how he treats a defenseless creature."

The man chuckled, his laugh like a warm brandy. "I'm lucky you're a librarian."

"And a farmer's daughter," I reminded him. "Tell me, Mr. Block. How is the little bitch now?"

Mr. Block—or perhaps the animal—made a strange sound. "Well, I just got her all nestled in a box, but I don't think she'll feel content until I'm holding her. Miss Novak," he said, in a most sincere voice, "could we rain-check until dinner?"

Frankly, I was a bit surprised by how polite he was being. So what could I say? I was hoping for a great deal from my relationship with Catcher Block. "Of course," I said graciously. "Good-bye, Mr. Block, until dinner."

I replaced the receiver, smiled at the waiter, who removed the phone, then explained the situation to Vikki and Mr. MacMannus.

At least we'd get to discuss my book with *KNOW Magazine*'s publisher, and have a delicious luncheon.

I do hope Catcher Block has a chance to nibble on something, I thought as I opened the huge menu the maître d' placed in my hands.

CATCHER

I hung up the phone, slipped my arm around my little English foxhound—a "little bitch" by the name of Gwendolyn—and nibbled on her ear until she was practically wagging her tail.

I had her nestled in a little box, all right—a private box at the theater for a matinee of the hottest show in town.

Oh, yeah. The play was a pretty hot show, too: *Camelot*, starring Robert Goulet, Julie Andrews, and Richard Burton.

But as the houselights went down and the overture began to play, my little flight attendant decided she found me to be a much more attractive leading man.

How could I hurt the poor girl's feelings? Giving in, I closed the velvet curtains. And then . . .

Well, you don't really expect me to go on, do you?

I may be a ladies' man, man's man, man-about-town, but I am a gentleman, after all.

At least in print.

Barbara

I was wearing a slim-fitting embroidered floor-length black-and-gold lace evening gown with jewel straps and full-length black gloves under a pink evening wrap. Vikki looked darling in a black matte jersey halter gown with a jeweled neck worn under a black silk evening wrap. We were dressed to the nines if I say so myself.

The maître d' took our wraps and then led us past the floor-to-ceiling glass walls through which we enjoyed a thrilling view of the sparkling New York City skyline. It was a magical night, a night full of promise. A perfect time and place for a dinner meeting with Catcher Block.

Mr. MacMannus was waiting for us at the table, looking quite cute in black tie. But he also looked rather distraught. Once again, he was alone.

And he was holding a courtesy phone. Looking like a helpless little boy, he held out the receiver to me.

I took the phone and cleared my throat. "This is Barbara Novak," I said evenly.

"Miss Novak, I'm so sorry, the darnedest thing . . ."

"Yes, Mr. Block?"

45

"I'm out in the park with my little French poodle, and she's just not ready to go in yet—if you know what I mean."

"Oh, I do," I said, struggling to overcome my impending sense of disappointment. "But here's a little advice from a farm girl to a city boy. You'll find if you stick a little twig in her bottom, she'll remember why she went out with you in the first place."

Mr. Block sounded as if he were choking. Or perhaps he was coughing. I hoped he wasn't catching cold spending all that time outdoors with dogs.

"I'll keep that in mind," he said at last. "Miss Novak, I hate to ask, but could we rain-check until breakfast?"

I sighed. What could I say? No matter what I was feeling—no matter what I wanted to say—I had to think of all my plans for *Down with Love*.

My success depended on Catcher Block.

"Of course," I said in what I hoped was a gracious tone of voice. "Good-bye, Mr. Block. Until breakfast."

I hung up, smiled at the waiter, and explained Mr. Block's excuse to Vikki and Mr. MacMannus. Then I opened my menu and tried to think about what to order. If Mr. Block couldn't get his pet to do what he wanted, maybe he needed a better chain. Or a toy, perhaps. Maybe what he needed was a good ball.

CATCHER

I hung up the phone with Barbara Novak and slipped my arm around my little "French poodle"—a charming stewardess named Yvette.

Now, believe me, I hadn't planned on standing Miss Novak up again. And I hadn't exactly lied to her. Yvette and I were at the park. The ballpark. Yankee Stadium, in fact, and, well, she just wasn't ready to go in yet.

I couldn't blame her. There was something invigorating about the terminology of a baseball game. I snuggled in for a few more kisses.

"Well! We have a base on balls!" shouted the announcer over the loudspeaker. "Everybody settle in. Looks like the start of a long doubleheader!"

I forgot about business and concentrated on the next home run.

Barbara

I don't remember what I wore to breakfast the next morning. Although I do seem to remember that Vikki wore her green silk jacquard sack dress with a darling little hat.

We'd met Mr. MacMannus at the Palm Court for brunch, just as planned. It was a beautiful morning, but by the time the waiter cleared away our meal, some of the joy had gone out of the rendezvous. Our conversation had dribbled away to nothing. We sat motionless, staring into space.

Catcher Block still hadn't come.

"I just don't know . . ." Mr. MacMannus was saying. "It's not like Catch to be late."

"No," I agreed. "He usually calls to cancel right on time."

"Barbara," Vikki said, placing a gentle hand on mine, "I'm sure he'll call."

I shot her a look.

"I mean, come."

I didn't answer. Things were not going according to plan, and I stared out into space, wondering what I should do now. I certainly enjoyed eating out at some of Manhattan's finest restaurants on Peter MacMannus's expense account. But if I wasn't careful, it would drive me to drink. As in Metrecal diet meal replacement, the working girl's liquid lunch.

This was getting me nowhere with Catcher Block.

As we sat there waiting, I began unintentionally to eavesdrop on the diners seated next to us.

"Elke and I missed you at lunch yesterday, Gwendolyn," one was saying.

"I took in a matinee," Gwendolyn said. "With Catcher Block."

GONG! A bell went off in my head and my eyes popped open.

"Is that so?" the first girl asked. She sounded as incensed as I felt.

"But Elke and I missed you at dinner last night, Yvette," Gwendolyn went on.

"I took in a night game," Yvette said, and burst into tears. "With Catcher Block!"

GONG! GONG!

I couldn't help it. I turned around in my seat and split the fanning palm that separated our two tables so I could get a better look.

Gwendolyn and Yvette were dressed in darling matching stewardess uniforms—and they were both drop-dead gorgeous.

"I told him I'd give up flying for him!" Gwendolyn sulked.

"I did, too!" Yvette complained. Her lower lip quivered. "Now I wonder if he ever loved me!"

"I wonder if he even cared!" Gwendolyn blubbered.

"I wonder what's keeping Elke!" they both sobbed.

I guess they were too weepy to wait—or perhaps they figured out that it was pointless waiting for a woman who was most likely in the arms of Catcher "Romeo" Block. Either way, they decided to skip breakfast and fled the restaurant just as a waiter approached my table with a courtesy phone.

Discourtesy was more like it, if the call was from Catcher Block. All those excuses he'd given me over the past two days—total fibs! The man ought to give up journalism and switch to fiction.

Oh, boy! I couldn't wait to give Mr. Block a piece of my mind! Steaming mad, I didn't even wait for Mr. MacMannus to answer. I seized the receiver and said, "This is Barbara Novak."

Anyone who can't recite the next line with me ought to get sent back to first grade.

"I'm so sorry, Miss Novak, darnedest thing . . ."

I actually looked forward to hearing what excuse he'd conceived of this time.

"I got waylaid by the sweetest Swedish Lapphund," he began. "She kept me up half the night, and I'm afraid I'm still in bed."

I just bet! And I could just imagine what his little Swedish lapdog was doing right now.

I opened my mouth to tell him off, when I remembered something. Didn't poor Gwendolyn and Yvette's missing friend have a Swedish-sounding name . . . ? Elke? Yes, that was it.

Apparently Catcher Block was addicted to more than the airlines' in-flight cocktail peanuts.

"My!" I exclaimed. "You do get *way*-laid."

But apparently he was too distracted at the moment to pick up on my sarcastic double entendre.

Someone was whispering to him in the background. It sounded like "Would you care for another beverage?"

Sounded like a stewardess to me!

"No, thank you," Mr. Block whispered quietly.

"I beg your pardon?" I prodded.

"Uh, I was saying . . . thank you, Miss Novak. You're very understanding."

"I understand everything, Mr. Block. A little advice?"

He chuckled. "From a farm girl to a city boy?"

But our polite little game of hide-and-seek was about to end. I didn't feel like playing by his rules anymore. "No," I replied hotly. "From a book author—*hardcover*—to someone who fills up the space in a magazine between the advertisements."

That got his attention.

The charm instantly evaporated. "How about some

advice from someone more experienced to—shall I say—a virgin?"

My mouth dropped open. I had never been spoken to so rudely in my life. At least, not by a man who wasn't my boss.

"This book you're so proud of seems a little passé, Miss Novak," he said in a patronizing tone of voice. "We gave women the vote over forty years ago. This is the Space Age. JFK says we'll be flying men to the moon soon."

"*Men* will be flying to the moon," I pointed out. "The only job a woman can get in the air is serving cocktails, and she can only get that job if she's thin, pretty, unmarried, under thirty, and doesn't wear glasses."

"So, the airlines wouldn't take you," he said pityingly. "That's no reason to disparage stewardesses."

Oooh! The *nerve* of that man! "*I'm* not the one disparaging them!" I shot back. "I'm all for working women. That's why I'm sending you several dozen copies of my book. You can keep them on your bedside table and give them away as parting gifts to the girls like—oh, I don't know—say, Elke, Yvette, and Gwendolyn!"

Did I just imagine it? Or did I hear the worm squirm? "Then they'll know who the real dog is," I went on, "and they'll stay committed to their careers!"

Catcher Block didn't even stumble. "Oh, they are committed. In fact, all three of them are flying out of here at noon. Mind if we rain-check until lunch?"

I could not believe that after all he'd said, after all he'd done, after all his *lies* and *insults* . . . he thought he could still twist me around his little finger and have his way with me, as if I were just another one of his little bonbons waiting in line to take a number.

Well, I'd not only written *Down with Love*, I'd *read* it. And it was time to practice what I preached.

"Mr. Block," I said, "you can take your rain check and—as we say on the farm at harvesttime—put it where the sun does not shine!"

"Miss Novak," he deadpanned, "if you're looking to get dinner, just say so."

I was thankful I was having this conversation in a public place. It prevented me from screaming at that moment at the top of my lungs.

"Mr. Block," I responded, "I wouldn't meet with you in a hundred years. Good-bye, Mr. Block. Forever!"

I hung up before he could reply.

Vikki and Mr. MacMannus were staring at me in disbelief.

I smiled and got up to leave. "Thank you for all your trouble, Mr. MacMannus."

He struggled to his feet. "Not at all," he croaked. Poor man. I'd enjoyed dining with him for the past few days. He was really quite sweet. Now he looked totally devastated, though I wasn't sure why.

"Vikki," I said, "I'll get us a taxi."

Later, in the taxi, Vikki confessed what was going on. And then it all became clear to me.

Apparently Peter MacMannus was desperate to have his top writer do an article on me—not because he was particularly interested in me or my book but because he was particularly interested in my editor.

Peter MacMannus was hopelessly in love with Vikki.

And Vikki definitely had feelings for him.

According to Vikki, their conversation after I left the table went something like this.

"I guess this means we're through," Peter muttered as Vikki pulled on her gloves.

"Sad, isn't it?" she replied. "This is the first time I've ever had to eliminate having a future with a man before we've even had a chance to have had a past." She stood and gave him a sad smile. "Good-bye, Mr. MacMannus."

With great regret, she left him slumped in the booth.

That's when I knew I'd found more than an editor in Vikki Hiller. I'd also found a best friend.

CATCHER

I'm a loyal kind of guy. No, really, no kidding. I'm loyal to every girl I meet every minute she's in my arms. And I also felt a certain sense of loyalty to my friend and boss, Peter MacMannus.

Though I've never gone in for guilt trips, I will say I felt a twinge of regret that my problems with the Novak chick had spilled over into Peter's love life. Or rather, his attempt to get one. But hey, it was a lesson learned. You should never hang your hat—or your heart—on just one doll's bedroom door.

So to ease my various twinges, I dragged my lovelorn pal off for some medicinal recreation at a dark, smoky, out-of-the-way place called the Astronette Club. (The souvenir security-clearance badge from the NASA luau got us in free.)

Now we were seated at one of those little round tables near the stage, where the floor show was about to begin, knocking back the house specialty, a mostly vodka concoction known as a Sputnik.

Peter was definitely in orbit.

"Hello, Peter," I coached. "Stay with me, buddy."

"It was nice while it lasted," he slurred. "I haven't had dinner and breakfast with the same woman since I had a nanny."

I shook my head. There was only one thing worse than a drunk—and that was a simpering, whimpering drunk.

I really had to do something about this guy, or I wouldn't be able to work for him.

That's why I brought him here. To show him a lush buffet of appetizers and desserts; convince him there was more than one dish on the menu.

"I'm sorry, Peter," I said firmly, "but Vikki's not the only girl for you. That's why I brought you here."

Right on cue there was a drumroll followed by a loud crash of the cymbals. Then the curtains jerked open, and out came a high-kicking chorus line of ladies in silver bikinis, little silver high-heeled boots, and astronaut-style helmets. And that was just the warm-up.

"You brought me here 'cause we're buddies, right?" Peter shouted over the music. "*Bosom* buddies!"

I wiped the spray off my face with a cocktail napkin, forgiving Peter because I knew he was just as heartbroken as he was plastered.

"Get a load of those rockets!" I said, trying to get his mind off Vikki.

"Here's to antigravity!" Peter howled. And his head fell with a bang on the table.

I lifted Peter's head by his hair and gave his cheeks a few light slaps—the same as I'd do for any man. "Stay with me or you'll get the spins," I warned him. "Whatever you do, don't close your eyes. Don't close your eyes . . . Don't close your eyes!"

Barbara

"C lose your eyes!" Vikki ordered that afternoon as we stepped out of another taxi.

After our disastrous brunch, I'd gone home and tried to cheer myself up by changing into my vintage yellow tweed slim-skirted suit, with the three-quarter-length jacket and green cotton collar vest.

When that didn't work, Vikki make a quick phone call, then told me she had a surprise for me. A quick trip across town and she was pulling me out onto the sidewalk, insisting that I keep my eyes closed tight.

Which made it a little hard to walk on a busy Manhattan street in heels.

I couldn't imagine what she could show me in a shop window that would cheer me up, but I decided, after all she'd done for me, to let her have her fun.

Don't tell her, but I peeked as we went in. I almost fainted when I saw President John F. Kennedy grinning at me from three feet away—then realized it was only a poster-size photo of him standing next to a huge blowup of the cover of his book *Profiles in Courage*.

That's when I began to get excited. I remembered the blowup that Maurice had done of the cover of *Down with Love*. And what about the photo shoot?

Could it be . . . ? Was I going to spend the night in Scribner's window with JFK?

But strangely enough, we didn't stop near the front of the store. I felt my editor leading me on, first down one aisle, then another, like mice in a maze.

My curiosity was piqued!

At last we stopped. I held my breath.

"Open your eyes!" Vikki cried. "Open your eyes!"

I opened my eyes and looked around.

We were at the back of the store, near the rest rooms. The only patrons in the entire section.

I didn't see my beautiful big pink cover, or the life-size photo of me in my snug pink suit. We were so far from the front of the store, I couldn't even see the president.

I looked at Vikki, a question in my eyes. Had she actually said "surprise"?

Vikki smiled broadly and pointed to a shelf next to the fire extinguisher. Small black letters on the edge of the shelf identified the section as CULTURAL STUDIES.

I frowned and shook my head in confusion.

She pointed at the spine of a book.

Please note: I said "*a* book." As in *one measly copy*.

If I turned my head completely sideways, I could read the words *Down with Love* in small pink type along the spine.

"Ta-da!" Vikki cried, with what I felt was rather forced enthusiasm. "It's your book! On sale! Scribner's Fifth Avenue!"

Poor Vikki. She'd worked her little behind off on this project, fought for it every step of the way, staked her career on it with the Banner House Fratboys. And now here she was playing head cheerleader at a losing game . . . for my sake.

But I couldn't help it. I was crestfallen. Did anyone ever come back here except to go to the bathroom or put out a fire?

Fighting back tears, I reached out and lovingly traced the single spine with a single gloved finger. "One?" I said softly. "Just one? All that work and . . . one?"

Vikki smiled cheerfully, as if *one* were a good number.

But her brave smile only made me feel worse. "If somebody buys this, there'll be . . . none." I tried to swallow the lump in my throat. "It will be as if it never existed."

"No, no!" Vikki rushed to reassure me.

I looked up hopefully.

"Doubleday also has one."

I guess she realized how pitiful that sounded. With a deep sigh, she linked arms with me, and together we walked out of the bookstore, dragging our purses behind us.

"See you later, Mr. President," I said with a little wave as I passed by the bookstore window.

We walked along Broadway in the Fifties, oblivious to

the sunshine of a beautiful day. Or at least, I was. Vikki was already planning her next move.

"Barbara," she began, "I know you're thinking this is a real setback. But I promise you. I'll think of something."

She stopped and looked up, a finger to her chin, as if she meant to think up something right then and there.

But then I realized she wasn't thinking—she was reading. Reading something above our heads.

I glanced up. The marquee of the famous Ed Sullivan Theater promised A REALLY BIG SHOW THIS SUNDAY.

"If only we could get your book on *The Ed Sullivan Show* . . ." Vikki mused.

"Yeah," I said wistfully. *The Ed Sullivan Show* was a variety show, and my favorite television program. You never knew what kind of act he'd have on next. Acrobats from China. A man spinning plates. Judy Garland, Frank and Dean. I'd even seen Elvis—at least from the waist up.

Singers, acrobats, dog tricks, puppets. But I'd never seen a book.

"How exactly do you get a *book* on *The Ed Sullivan Show*?" I wondered.

Vikki grinned, and I could see the wheels turning in her head. Now that she'd gone head-to-head with the Banner House Fratboys, she was ready to take on the world.

Barbara

I couldn't believe it! Vikki and I were backstage at the Ed Sullivan Theater! It was a little strange, watching live from the wings instead of watching it on the tiny black-and-white screen of a TV set. The acrobatic-bear family spinning plates kept stepping on the hem of my evening gown.

But I didn't care.

"Vikki, you're incredible!" I whispered excitedly. "I can't believe you got Judy Garland to sing a song of my book on *The Ed Sullivan Show*!"

"Isn't it the most!" Vikki said.

"She wasn't even on the bill!" I reminded her. "How did they fit her into the lineup?"

"The best luck!" Vikki confided. "The Singing Nun fell off her scooter coming across the Triborough Bridge." She glanced up at heaven and winked. "I guess somebody up there likes me!"

Just then the producer called for quiet. We were coming back live from a commercial. We waited breathlessly until he gave Mr. Sullivan his cue.

"Tonight, ladies and gentlemen, we have a really big surprise," Mr. Sullivan announced. "To coincide with the arrival of the new book *Down with Love* in bookstores this week from coast to coast, here's a special friend of our show to sing you a song of that book—Judy Garland!"

Vikki and I squealed—very quietly, of course. Mr. Sullivan often scolded the teenagers who squealed for their teen idols, and threatened to stop the show.

We held up both hands with our fingers crossed.

And then there she was—standing in this crazy pink set of hanging arrows right off the cover of my book!

I listened to her sing, humming the tune under my breath. While she was getting down with everything romantic and stupid, I was getting down to the rhythm of the big-band orchestra. Meanwhile, my spirits were soaring at the thought of Dorothy from *The Wizard of Oz* singing a song named after my very own book!

When Judy finished, she blew us a kiss. Vikki and I jumped up and down, applauding like mad!

The Ed Sullivan Show was seen all over America and in countries all over the world.

I wondered if it would make a difference in my book sales.

∗

It didn't take long to find out.

The next day Vikki and I learned that the network switchboard lit up the moment Judy took her bow. Women

63

all over America had stopped in the middle of serving Sunday-night TV dinners to call—they wanted to know where they could find my book.

Before the week was out, I'd made it to the top of the *New York Chronicle* Bestseller List: No. 1: *Down with Love*, by Barbara Novak.

Vikki and I celebrated with champagne. They packed up poor old cardboard JFK and replaced him with a life-size cutout of . . . ME.

In my hot-pink suit.

Everything was beginning to fall into place.

Are you paying attention to me now, Catcher Block?

CATCHER

Damn!

Pardon my French. (Or perhaps Vikki will have edited it out.)

But there was no other word for how I was feeling.

Peter and I were at the barbershop getting haircuts, which usually made me feel on top of my game.

But it was going to take more than a trim and a shoeshine to brighten my day.

Not even the *Mad* magazine I was reading could cheer me up. Alfred E. Neuman, dressed in a blond wig and pink suit, grinned at me over the cover of a pink book with the words WHAT, ME WORRY? emblazoned on a *Down with Love*–like arrow.

Everywhere I looked I saw pictures of Barbara Novak grinning at me like some mischievous pussycat. And the worst part of it was? She was one good-looking dame.

"You said she was a spinster!" I accused Peter.

"I never used the word *spinster* in my life!" he complained. Then why wouldn't he look at me? Why was he hiding behind that copy of the *Wall Street Journal*?

"Okay, once: when I told my mother that it was technically incorrect for her to call her son a spinster."

Hardly a confession. But there was more. "You said she was a brunette!" I reminded him.

"I did not!"

He's in denial, I thought. *Or maybe it's me.*

"She sure didn't sound like a blonde on the phone," I muttered at last.

And then I knew what I had to do. "You still want to date Vikki?"

The *Wall Street Journal* came down. I had Peter's full attention. "Of course I do! You think I want to die a spinster?"

"Call her," I told him. "Tell her I'll do the cover."

"Oh, Catch! You're the best friend a guy—"

"Just call," I said. No need for him to thank me. I had my own reasons for agreeing to interview Barbara Novak.

Barbara

The next morning Theodore Banner ordered Vikki and me to meet at his office. *Down with Love* was such an important event in the history of Banner House Publishing, he wanted photographs for the company archives.

Banner was so full of it, he had to make a speech.

"Not since Johannes Gutenberg's invention of the printing press allowed for the wide dissemination of the greatest thoughts of man to reach the masses, forever changing the landscape of human destiny, has one book reached so many and achieved so much, reminding all of us here today of the noble goal that called us to dedicate our lives to toil in the field of publishing to begin with—*sales!*"

Mr. Banner kept hugging Vikki and me—I'm not sure how much of that had to do with book sales—and we toasted with champagne. "Here's to Banner House's new number one author and our new number one editor!"

No one said anything.

I glanced at the staff. Vikki and I were the only women in the room. She and I stood out like tropical birds against the sea of dark suits.

To his credit, Theodore Banner glared at his staff. "Say 'cheers,' everybody!" It was an order, not a request.

"Cheers," E.G., C.B., C.W., J.B., J.R., and R.J. muttered quite unenthusiastically from where they stood in a sullen little mob behind the photographer.

I stifled a giggle. The men looked ready to spit paper clips!

But Vikki looked positively radiant. As well she should. She'd pulled off nothing short of a miracle.

"Hold on! One more!" the photographer called out.

Mr. Banner snatched up his ukulele. "How's that Judy Garland song go again, B.N.?" He started strumming, singing way too fast, like something out of an old Rudy Vallee movie. "'After you've gone and left me crying, After you've gone there's no denying—'"

"No, no, T.B.," I said, choking back my laughter. "It's 'Down with Love.'"

He looked puzzled. "I don't know that one." Then he shrugged, completely unfazed, as only the rich and powerful can be, then started strumming his old vaudeville tune again. "'You'll feel blue, you'll feel sad, you'll miss the bestest pal you ever had—'"

By now the senior editors—the male ones—appeared ready to riot, so Vikki and I excused ourselves, saying we had some important business to take care of with respect to the book.

Stifling our snickers, we teetered down the hallway as

quickly as we could in our heels and escaped into Vikki's office—then burst into total fits of laughter.

What a triumph! What sweet, delicious success! Eve's earth-shattering bite of the apple in the Garden of Eden couldn't have tasted any more divine than our bite into the Big Apple.

It didn't hurt one bit that we were celebrating in Vikki's *new* office.

What an improvement over the tiny interior closet they'd stuck her in before! Her new office was spacious, beautifully decorated, with a corner window and an unbelievably fantastic view. I wondered if one of the alphabet editors had had to give it up to make room for Banner House Publishing's "new number one editor."

"Those men are livid—'B.N.'!" she crowed. "You're a hit! You're bigger than the pill!"

"Oh, talk about big, 'V.H.,'" I gushed. "This office is *huge!* Congratulations!" I squealed, clinking champagne glasses with her again. "We did it!"

You can't imagine how we felt. We were so giddy, we even considered asking a secretary to make *us* coffee! We had a good laugh over that, but then decided, just for today, we didn't want anything to interfere with the champagne.

There was a knock at the door, and we quickly tried to school our features to look serious and busy, but then relaxed when we saw that it was just Gladys, our comrade-in-arms.

And I was stunned by the change in her. She'd had a total makeover, and looked every inch the smart, sophisticated career gal. "Hel-lo, Gladys!" I exclaimed. "You look wonderful!"

She blushed in delight and shrugged. "As you told me, Barbara, 'it's never too late.'" She patted her hair with such dignity and pride, I suddenly had an overwhelming sense of fulfillment.

Yes, *The Ed Sullivan Show* was exciting. The book sales, the publicity, the champagne . . . the senior editors' chagrin . . . it was all a big thrill.

But here in the flesh was the real success. An ordinary working girl who'd read my book and taken its advice to heart. Who'd taken charge of her life.

That was the real thrill. The genuine victory.

And best of all, Vikki and I had achieved this on our own—without riding the coattails of some man.

Without Catcher Block's precious prose.

"Vikki," Gladys said then, interrupting my thoughts, "Peter MacMannus called again." She chuckled. "Now it's every hour."

My editor and I exchanged a look.

But we didn't have to say a word.

"Tell him we're too busy," we both said at that same moment—and then, laughing like best friends at a slumber party, we topped off our champagne.

CATCHER

What do you mean, 'too busy'?" I asked Peter, and jabbed the button in my apartment that activates the bar. A panel opened and it rolled out to the rescue.

"You know what it means," Peter said, opening a silver shaker and filling it with ice for martinis. "They hate us."

I went to the closet and shrugged out of my jacket and tie. "Too busy," I griped. "Huh. Kennedy, Khrushchev, and Castro weren't too busy during the Cuban Missile Crisis to sit down and talk to me. But this *Down with Love* chick is 'too busy.' Doing what? Eating chocolate?"

I punched the remote control, turning on the TV. It was time for *Guess My Game*, the show that pitted blindfolded celebrities against one another trying to guess the occupation of that week's Mystery Guest.

You'll never guess whose face filled the screen.

Peter dropped the glass swizzler in the martini pitcher. "It's Novak!"

"Shh!" I said.

She was the Mystery Guest!

The celebrity panelists were just taking off their masks

and the audience was clapping wildly. For once, the enthusiasm didn't sound canned.

"Barbara," said the emcee with the wide, toothy grin. "I know every woman bought your book, and I know every man sneaked out and bought it just to find out what their women were reading."

"That's why sales doubled," Barbara said. She sounded confident. Too confident, if you asked me. I thought she looked smug.

"But then they tripled!" the emcee pointed out. "How did *that* happen?"

"Actually, that's a very funny story," she replied, obviously wallowing in the attention. "It seems church groups in the Bible Belt were so zealous about being *seen* burning my book that every time they had a bonfire they would call up the next day and reorder so they could have another one!"

Everyone on TV laughed and clapped.

Glowering, I pulled off my shirt.

"I've heard a lot of talk about chapter eight," the emcee went on in his tinny voice, "about the worst kind of man, the kind all women should avoid. What's that title again?"

Miss Novak smiled knowingly. "Oh, yes. It's called 'Men Who Change Women As Often As They Change Their Shirts.'"

Bare-chested, reaching for a fresh French-cuff shirt, I froze and stared.

The emcee chuckled as only an emcee can. "And have you met a lot of that kind of man in your research?"

"You're not asking me to name names, are you?" Barbara said, batting her eyes flirtatiously.

"No," the emcee said, "of course not—"

"Catcher Block," she blurted.

Well, thank you very much, Miss Novak! I thought. I felt the blood drain from my face. *Catcher Block, the Man Who Changes Women As Often As He Changes His Shirt.* There you had it, live, on national TV, straight from the author of *Down with Love*, the great Barbara Novak!

"Wow." Peter guffawed. "Four million women in the naked city, and the one you let get away, the one you had to get on the bad side of, is the woman all the other four million are listening to!"

I fired the remote at the TV and the picture died. Peter, my supposed friend, somehow found this *amusing*.

"You blew it, buddy!" he crowed. "The Age of Catcher Block, ladies' man, man's man, man-about-town, is *over*! The king is *dead*!"

I pushed the button that sent the bar back into the wall. "I hate to spoil your fun, Mac," I growled, "but the four million women I go out with aren't listening to Barbara Novak."

The phone rang and I snatched up the receiver. "Yes?" I barked. Then my module got an instant rocket booster. "Gwendolyn!"

Her timing couldn't have been more perfect. I needed a woman—a real woman—to help me forget. Cradling the phone on my shoulder, I removed a clean shirt from the laundry box on the couch. "Where are you, baby?"

"At the airport."

"Well, get out of the airport," I scolded playfully. "We have reservations for ten o'clock."

Then she dropped a bombshell. Not the good kind.

She wasn't coming.

Peter was watching me closely over the rim of his martini glass. I turned away. "But you can't sit in the terminal until three A.M.," I argued, then added suggestively, "Aren't you going to get . . . 'hungry'?"

I heard her munching on something, something that sounded gooey, like . . .

Chocolate.

"No, I'm pretty full," she answered around a mouthful. "Besides," she went on, "I have to catch up on some reading."

"Reading?!" I exclaimed in disbelief. Did I have the right Gwendolyn? What kind of book would a girl like dear sweet Gwendolyn need to be reading? More important, what kind of book would dear, sweet Gwendolyn possibly be reading instead of spending the night with Catcher Block?

Then she told me the title.

My heart sank like the *Titanic*.

"Good night, Gwendolyn," I said, and hung up the phone. I would have thrown it out the window except for the fact that I'd be needing it later, to line up a date to replace Gwendolyn.

"What's the matter, Catch," Peter quipped, "lose another one?"

I scowled, wondering if he could hear the war drums that had begun pounding in my brain.

This thing was spreading like a virus. Somebody needed to come up with a cure—before it was too late.

I nominated myself.

"I'm going to bury Novak and turn this crazy upside-*Down-with-Love* world right side up again." I began to pace, planning my story. "I'm going to write the exposé of the century, and the world will learn once and for all that deep down inside all women are the same. They all want the same thing: love and marriage. Even Miss Barbara *Down with Love* Novak. And I'm going to prove it!"

"How?" Peter asked, playing the Innocent Man. "Novak won't even see you."

"That's right," I said. "That's why Novak won't even see me coming."

I ripped off the fresh shirt I was wearing, tossed it over my shoulder, and grabbed another from the laundry box.

Barbara

Everyone wanted a piece of Barbara Novak.

I was one of the most successful women in America. Maybe in the world. People stopped me in the streets, begging me to autograph their little pink books. Insisting I listen as they shared their stories of how I'd changed their lives.

They wanted me for the *Today* show. The evening news. At cross-stitch conventions and women's-club brunches. I'd been on the cover of every magazine from *Ladies' Home Journal* to *TV Guide*. ABC, NBC, the BBC—they all wanted my time.

Everyone wanted Barbara Novak, the bestselling author.

But nobody wanted Barbara Novak, the woman.

It was true.

My true confession, dear reader, is that in a world where women were calling the shots in the sexual Olympics, I was still sitting home without a date for the prom.

I was successful. But I was lonely.

When a gal feels like this, there's only one thing to do. Dive into the nearest bed.

In your rattiest pj's . . . with a good book.

And that was exactly what I was going to do.

I had just put on my favorite Chinese silk pajamas when the doorbell rang.

I slipped into my slides, tossed on the matching Chinese silk robe, and hiked across the sunken living room to answer it. Of course I stole a look through the peephole first to see who it was, hoping . . .

But it was just Vikki. With a sigh, I opened the door.

She looked simply divine in a new fur coat draped over an exquisite floor-length evening gown—the look marred only by her shocked expression.

"Barbara! You're not dressed!" she exclaimed. "Aren't you coming?"

"No," I said casually. "I'm just going to stay in tonight."

She blinked. "Why? Because you don't have a date?"

I shrugged, as if it were no big deal.

With a tinkling laugh, she breezed past me into the apartment, ready to help me throw some little outfit together. "My date's a quarterback with twenty-seven teammates. I'm *sure* he could fix you up."

What a sweetheart, I thought. She still hadn't figured it out.

"I'm sure he *couldn't*," I said bluntly. "I am persona non grata to all men."

Her face was still a blank.

How much clearer could I put it? "I can't even get picked up by a taxi driver!" I exclaimed.

Vikki's hand flew to her mouth, and her eyes shone briefly with pity.

I had turned the world of sex and dating upside down. I'd rallied enslaved women everywhere to rise up against their masculine masters and make their own rules. Women adored me. I was their heroine. Their fearless leader.

Men wouldn't touch me with a ten-foot pole. Or anything else, for that matter.

Vikki took my hands in hers, studying my face with concern. "This is crazy. All this fame and success—and Miss Sex à la Carte is the only woman who can't have sex à la carte?"

Laughing softly, I dabbed at the corner of my eye with the cuff of my Chinese silk sleeve. "At least not on this earth."

Vikki's eyes lit up. Like a twenty-four-hour deli, her brain never closed. "Maybe we should find an astronaut who's been in orbit the past two weeks," she suggested.

I just shook my head and smiled at her with affection. Was there anything this brilliant editor wouldn't do for her first-time author? She really was a chum.

But I had to get control of myself. Really, we were both missing the point here. What had I spent months advising other women to do?

I was pitiful. An embarrassment. A fake!

If I couldn't take my own advice from *Down with Love*, how could I expect my readers to?

I squared my shoulders and gave my biggest fan my most cheerful smile. "It's all right, Vikki," I said confidently. "I'm perfectly content on my own."

She bought it, and returned the smile. "Well, when it comes to not needing a man, you wrote the book!" she joked, totally cracking herself up.

I laughed along with her. And it was a wonderful *Down with Love* moment—two independent women, laughing at outdated convention, in charge of their own destiny—on top of the world.

"Have fun with your quarterback, Vikki," I ordered as I ushered her out the door. "And remember, *you* call the plays."

Vikki winked, then glided down the hallway to the elevator, humming the *Down with Love* anthem. I watched her go, then slowly closed the door.

Congratulations on your Academy Award–winning performance, I told myself. I'd convinced Vikki I was fine.

Now if I could only convince myself.

Giving myself a mental shake, I marched across the living room and curled up on my comfy designer couch.

I mean, come on. Most women in the world were scrubbing burned pot roast off roasting pans or changing diapers right about now. I was one of the lucky ones—I had no one to pick up after, no one to cook for, no one to answer to but myself. I could do whatever I pleased.

Not only that, I had an exquisite luxury apartment to do

it in, with a fantastic view of the Manhattan skyline at night . . .

Beneath a beautiful . . . romantic . . . full moon . . .

Read! That's what I wanted to do. I was a writer. Writers write and writers read.

I snatched up a magazine from the coffee table and skimmed the cover lines.

It was the latest *KNOW Magazine.* (Don't tell anyone, but I've been a subscriber for some time.) On the cover was a collage of an astronaut in a *Sieg heil* pose, arm pointed to the moon. And the words: MACH SCHNELL TO THE MOON by . . .

Catcher Block.

I scowled and tossed the magazine across the room.

"I read at the library," I muttered, and grabbed for a piece of chocolate from a half-empty box on the coffee table.

"Do your stuff, small, dark, and chocolate," I said, and stuffed it in my mouth.

I was the luckiest girl in the world, I told myself. I ate my chocolate and gazed at the moon.

And tried to ignore the name Catcher as it pounded in my brain to the rhythm of my aching heart.

CATCHER

The next day I stood on a street corner, gripping my steaming wiener and scowling at the world.

Nothing helped me get in touch with my inner man like eating lunch at a street-corner hot-dog stand. A dog with all the works. The heartburn would give me back my edge.

Peter abstained. But he didn't abstain from sharing his innermost feelings with me.

"My analyst made me realize that this entire episode with Vikki has taken quite a toll," he was saying. "Been quite the ordeal. Extremely debilitating. So he's going to Barbados for three months to recover."

Fascinating . . . Maybe I needed to go somewhere and bet on a fight.

I swallowed the last bite of my lunch, tossed the paper napkin into a green metal trash can, and then stepped into the avenue to wave down a taxi.

"Wait a minute," Peter said. "I have to pick up my dry cleaning."

"Can't," I said, irritated by his assumption that he could

tell me where to go, just because he gave me an outrageous salary, a sumptuous office, an unlimited expense account, and carte blanche with most of my stories. "Got to get back to the office. Skip in Research is doing a fact-check on Novak: who she knows, where she goes, what she likes for dinner, what she likes 'à la carte.'"

The driver was waiting.

"Two minutes!" Peter complained. "I waited for you to eat your hot dog."

I opened the curbside door of the cab and turned to give Peter a good-bye salute.

Then froze in my tracks.

The author of *Down with Love* had just turned the corner under an armload of laundry. A woman selling flowers waved a book at her, and the Novak babe stopped to autograph it. The flower lady! Was no one immune from Barbara Novak's spell?

As much as I hated her, I had to admit that standing there among the flowers under a load of laundry, Barbara Novak was a good-looking woman. Damned good-looking. Which gave me a beautifully wicked idea.

The cabbie honked his horn.

"You're right, Mac," I told Peter. "*I'll* pick up your cleaning. You go to the office."

I didn't wait for him to figure it out. I just snatched the laundry ticket from his fingers, pushed him into the cab, and waved the driver on.

While Barbara Novak basked in the adoration of the flower lady, I slipped into the laundry and prepared to ambush her.

A bell over the door tinkled as I went in, and a man and woman straight from Central Casting for "old-world couple" stepped out of the back room to wait on me.

"I'm getting it," the man said crabbily. "You iron!"

"No, you iron!" the old lady lobbed back. "And *I'll* spend all day up front kibitzing with the customers! We're equal now!"

I had a feeling that this woman was under the influence. Under the influence of a certain bestseller!

"Oy! Again with that book!" the man confirmed, but he was whipped. Sadly I watched him turn with his tail between his legs and scamper into the back room.

Disgusting! And it steeled my resolve to go through with my plan.

The wife ambled up to the counter, confiscated Peter's laundry ticket, and examined it suspiciously. I prayed everything was in order; the last thing I wanted to do was show her some ID. Then the front door opened again behind me, and the old lady responded to the bell with the kind of eagerness you'd expect from one of Pavlov's dogs.

"Hello, Novick!" the old walrus barked happily.

"Hello, Mrs. Litzer," Barbara Novak replied. "Where is Mr. Litzer?"

The lady of the house winked conspiratorially and jabbed a thumb in the direction of the dungeon.

Novak shot her a thumbs-up.

"Irving!" the woman yelled. "Say hello to Novick!"

The man poked his head around the curtain. "Hello, Novick," he said wearily.

"I'll get your things, dear," Mrs. Litzer told the famous author. Then she glared at me as if I were responsible for all her misfortunes. "Yours, too, mister."

Like practically every other New Yorker, I'd learned, in public places at least, to live within my own personal space. For Barbara Novak and me to be thrown together in a tiny alcove and neither say nor do anything that acknowledged the presence or the existence of each other was perfectly normal and acceptable behavior.

So it probably came as a mild surprise when I turned to her and spoke. Or maybe not, since I spoke to her as an out-of-towner.

"Pardon me, ma'am," I said in an exaggerated drawl—a bastardized version of an accent I'd found charming on the lips of a past girlfriend from Texas. Or was it Oklahoma? One of those aw-shucks cowboy states. "But you sure look familiar. Are you . . . ?"

Barbara nodded without a second thought. She was getting used to being recognized. "Yes, I am."

"Well, I'll be a monkey's uncle!" I hollered. "Wait till I tell the folks back home I took my clothes to the same dry cleaner as Miss Kim Novak, the famous Hollywood actress!"

She laughed. "No, no. I'm not *Kim* Novak. I'm *Barbara* Novak."

"Oh." I acted disappointed, then folded my arms and rubbed my chin like Roy Rogers at a Senate committee hearing. Then I shook my head. "That doesn't ring a bell."

But something definitely rang in *her* mind.

"You mean you've never heard of me?" she gasped.

I tried to look distressed. "I'm sorry, ma'am."

"Don't be," she said, brushing a lock of hair off her forehead. International female body language for *Take me, I'm yours!* "I find it very refreshing."

The dry-cleaning woman returned and handed me a little brown paper bag with a laundry ticket stapled to one side. "You, Mr. Absentminded Professor!" she scolded. "You left a lot of things in your pockets!" Then she left again.

I peeked in the bag.

"But . . . um, excuse me," Barbara Novak continued, finding my ignorance fascinating, to say the least. "Do you mean to tell me you've never heard of my book, the worldwide sensation *Down with Love*?"

"No, ma'am," I answered like a helpless idiot. But I had an excuse. I'd just thought of it. "I have not. But lately I've been out of this world." I peered into the bag and pretended to be surprised. "Oh! My NASA security badge! I've been looking all over for that!"

Ding! That time I could almost hear the bell go off in her head.

"You're an astronaut?" she exclaimed. "Really? Perhaps *I've* heard of *you*. What's your name?"

My eyes darted sideways, searching for ideas. I spotted a handwritten sign that said ZIPPERS REPAIRED.

"Zip," I said.

"Zip . . . ?"

Another sign told me the Litzers were MARTINIZING SPECIALISTS.

"Martin. Major Zip Martin."

Barbara Novak was beginning to find me delightful. "Tell me, Major. Are the parties in Cocoa Beach as wild and uncivilized as they look?"

"Oh, I can't say, ma'am," I drawled bashfully. "I'm not much for going to parties." I removed a pair of Peter's glasses from the bag and put them on. "My idea of a good time is to sit down with a good book and smoke my pipe." Lucky for me Peter had left a pipe in his coat pocket, so I took it out and bit it and held my face cocked just so, with my arms folded and my hand grasping my chin.

Miss Novak looked me over the way a rancher considers a steer and obviously liked what she saw.

Her eyes widened, and I swear I heard that bell again.

Mrs. Litzer hurried out and hung two orders of dry cleaning up by the cash register. "Pay later!" she shouted over her shoulder as she disappeared again. "Irving's burning the iron!"

Miss Novak and I reached for our dry cleaning and came away with our hangers tangled. I couldn't have planned it better myself.

"We're hooked!" Barbara said, laughing.

"I'll fix it," I offered gallantly. I untangled the hangers and handed Miss Novak her things. "There you go." Then I opened the door and we stepped outside.

It was a beautiful day—the sky above the rooftops was Riviera blue, and the trees were so green they looked dyed. "Well, good-bye," I said shyly, starting to get comfortable with my made-up accent, and turned away.

Damn, I was good at this!

"Zip!" Barbara called.

Quickly I wiped the smile off my face and turned around. "Yes?"

"You have my slip."

Through the clear film of the dry-cleaning bag I saw that indeed I was in possession of a very enticing long pink silk slip. What luck! The game had just started and I already had full possession of her underwear. I hadn't blushed since I was thirteen, but I did my best to act embarrassed. "I'm so sorry, ma'am," I said, averting my eyes. "My mistake."

"Don't blame yourself," Barbara said. "Maybe it's a Freudian slip."

As Zip Martin, I didn't get it, of course. So I just smiled blankly as I returned her undergarment and dipped a quick bow. "Maybe. Well, good-bye again," I said, and turned and walked away.

One. I knew this wasn't going to take longer than a ten-count.

Two. I understood the pressure she was under. Watching me walk away, knowing there was a chance I was walking out of her life . . . forever.

Three. I had it all, of course. I was handsome, intelligent, shy, wore clean clothes, and had a good job with the government.

Four. Not to mention the fact that I was completely unaware of her worldwide reputation as a shrill, self-centered, domineering man-hater.

F—

"Zip!"

Barbara Novak, down on the count of four! That had to be some kind of record. I turned, feigning surprise. "Yes, Miss Novak?"

"I don't suppose you're *staying* in New York?" she practically pleaded.

"Why, yes, I am," I said. "NASA sent me here to work on a special project." Then I walked back to her and whispered, "A *top secret* project."

"Oh?"

"Can you keep a secret?" I said.

"Yes."

"Me, too," I said, smiling. "Gee. It sure seems like we have a lot in common."

I could tell that last line nearly knocked her socks off. I mean, stockings, I corrected, glancing down at her shapely gams.

Miss Novak gave me a coy smile. "Why, yes, it does. Might be nice to see just what we have in common and what we have that's different."

I managed to respond with a baffled stare. It was hard, but I did it. "I'm sorry?"

"Would you like to go to my place," she said, "get to know each other a little better?"

"A *little* better?" I asked.

"A *lot* better," Barbara said, hoping I might be catching on finally.

I scratched my head like Li'l Abner in the funny papers. "A lot better than what?" I asked, dashing her hopes.

Very distinctly she pronounced the words, "*All the way* better."

"Oh! Gee!" I said, letting her know that even us farm-bred boys understand that kind of talk. "Oh, no, ma'am. I couldn't do that. I couldn't get to know you *all the way* better until I knew you much, much better."

"Well, I wouldn't want to wait too long," she said. "I

have no interest in falling in love. Do you think you know me well enough to let me buy you a drink?"

With a big wholesome smile I offered her my arm, and together we walked back down the street, past the dry cleaner, where I caught a glimpse of Mrs. Litzer peeking out the window watching us with great suspicion.

Barbara

Meanwhile, Vikki was having some problems of her own.

If she thought the all-male senior editorial staff was hard to work with before her success with *Down with Love*, it was nothing compared with how "Down with Vikki" they were afterward.

She thought she'd have an equal place at the conference table now—after all, she'd earned it.

But what she found out was that the all-male senior editorial staff not only didn't want to give her an equal place, they didn't want her at the table at all.

Every manuscript she proposed, they shot down.

"I don't think that's for Banner House, Vikki," E.G. said. "Sounds like a loser."

"Fine," Vikki said in exasperation, trying to retain her professional demeanor. "So Banner House is passing on Betty Friedan's *The Feminine Mystique* and Helen Gurley Brown's *Sex and the Single Girl*."

No matter what she proposed, they shot it down. Seething, she tossed out another title, as a test, just to see if she was perhaps imagining their hostility. "Next. I have a manuscript written by God with an introduction by John Glenn—"

"No, no," E.G. said, looking out the window. "Not really for us."

"I didn't think so," Vikki said.

CATCHER

*L*ose another pair of glasses?" I asked Peter when we met for a late lunch. The way he was holding the Mahogany menu, I couldn't tell if he was reading it or smelling it.

"No. I'm keeping a low profile," he explained. "Vikki's over there with some guy." He nodded toward one of the other tables.

It was Vikki, all right, only she was not just with "some guy."

"That's Johnny Trementus, the quarterback," I told him, as anyone but Peter would know. He gave me a blank look. "As in football," I said. Still nothing. "An American sport."

"Yeah, yeah," Peter said. He knew all about football. His family owned one of the NFL teams. "Back to Trementus. Is he big?"

"He's not huge, but he's good. Fourteen hundred and thirty-two complete passes."

Peter peeked over the menu and glared. "I wonder if he's going for fourteen hundred and thirty-three."

Trementus scanned the room, looking for something, just a waiter probably, but it sent Peter plunging back to his hiding place behind the menu.

I watched the object of Peter's affections and her over-bulked date. Vikki was leaning close to Johnny with an unlit cigarette dangling from her lips. Matches. That's what he was looking for. The quarterback patted his coat pockets, then searched around the candle on the table for something he could use to light her up.

"Well, Vikki's leaving herself wide open," I reported to Peter, "but Trementus, surprisingly, fumbles."

"What does that mean in layman's terms?" Peter asked from behind the menu.

Johnny stood up and gave Vikki a friendly hug, then headed for the exit alone. Whatever he'd said or done, Vikki clearly wasn't happy about it.

"He's leaving," I told Peter. "Now's your chance. Not only is she unguarded, she's injured. Replace him."

Peter put his elbow on the table and propped up his forehead. "I can't go over there. She hates me."

"She doesn't hate you," I argued. "She hates me. Stop warming the bench and get in the game."

"You really think I should?"

"It's now or never. Once you run my Novak exposé, she *will* hate you and the clock will have run out."

Peter glared at me. "Well, that's just great! Can't you get off your Novak warpath?"

"Nope. I've got her surrounded. And it won't take a surprise attack to enter her tepee. I'm telling you, Kimo Sabe, you want big wampum, make Vikki love you now."

Peter rolled his eyes. "Okay! Enough with the football talk! I'm going!"

I watched him go. *Poor guy*, I thought. He approached Vikki's table with all the confidence of a seventh grader at his first school dance.

Due to my extensive experience with lips, I was able to follow their conversation.

Peter stepped up to Vikki's table as she was lighting her own cigarette.

"Hello, Vikki." Good, Peter. Nice and cool.

"Hello, Peter."

But then Peter cracked like Humpty Dumpty. "Are you in love with that football player?" he blurted out.

I cringed. Poor guy just couldn't do cool.

"Not anymore!" she told him, on the verge of tears. "He only wanted one thing!" She held up a thick folder. "To slip me his manuscript! And he didn't even have the professional courtesy to try and seduce me first! I'm finished! As an executive and as a woman! The men who resent my success won't give me the time of day, and the men who respect my success won't give me the time of night!"

Peter slipped into the booth beside her and took her hand like a man about to propose. "I don't know about other men," he said sincerely. "But I swear, if I had the chance, I'd respect you and resent you night and day and day and night!"

Vikki looked surprised. "Oh, Peter! You would?"

"You bet!" he said sincerely.

Vikki beamed. "You're on!"

She raised her glass. He raised Johnny's. *Clink!*

Touchdown!

I shook my head. The poor slob had terrible form. But somehow he managed to score.

The maître d' came over with a scotch on the rocks for me. "Here you are, Mr. Block." I was grateful; I could use a drink. Coaching was hard work.

"Thanks, Henri. Only from now on"—I pulled Peter's spare glasses out of my pocket and slipped them on—"I'll be going by the name Major Zip Martin. Spread the word to the other maître d's . . . and the doormen, the theater ushers, the taxi drivers . . ."

Henri didn't even blink. "Done," he said simply. "*Major.*"

We go way back, Henri and I. All the way back to Candy and Claudette. I raised my glass in thanks.

Barbara

At last—I was getting "down with love."

Writing the advice was one thing. Living the advice was another.

But now that I'd put a little Zip in my love life, I was finally getting where I wanted to be. And if I handled things right, I might just be able to manipulate the whole affair without getting my heart broken.

Clink!

I toasted the night with champagne and studied Zip over my glass as I took a sip, the bubbles tickling my nose.

This was more like it. Champagne in a private Broadway theater box with a marvelous-looking man. All the fun with none of the fuss. And if I felt like ending the night with a little sex à la carte, well, I was in charge of the menu.

"Oh, Zip, isn't this exciting?" I murmured. "We must be the only two people in New York who haven't seen *Camelot* yet." I smiled up at him, admiring how honest and intelligent he looked in his glasses. "You're not just being nice? You really haven't seen it, either?"

Zip gazed down at me with one hand in the air. "I can honestly say I've never *seen* this show."

Something about the way he said it made me want to laugh, but I wasn't sure why.

Before I could wonder about it, the houselights dimmed and the audience settled into their seats.

I'd never seen a show from a private box, and it was definitely wreaking havoc with my imagination. Glancing sideways, I shifted in my seat to move a little closer to my date.

Zip smiled and shifted in his own seat . . . to lean forward with his chin on the railing.

Not exactly what I had hoped for, but I couldn't help smiling. How sweet. He was actually going to watch the play.

Unlike some men, who, under cover of the box's privacy, would have probably made it to third base by now.

Zip Martin was playing the game by his own rules.

But so was I—and I was definitely going to have fun playing the game.

✳

The next few weeks were more wonderful than I ever could have imagined. I saw Zip Martin almost every night. And we went everywhere. Rockefeller Center. Macy's at Herald Square. The UN building, the Automat, the Statue of Liberty.

Then came the nights, the glorious neon-studded nights.

Dylan at Folk City. Peter, Paul and Mary at the Village Gate. Streisand at Bon Soir.

Times Square, Roseland, the Latin Quarter, Pigalle. We heard Buddy Rich and Count Basie at the Metropole. We twisted in a twist contest at Smalls' Paradise.

So many places I almost ran out of outfits.

One night we were watching the stars over Central Park, a perfect place for romance.

Which meant it was time for me to make a move.

I was wearing one of my favorite dresses, a strapless magenta chiffon gown with a swath of Wedgwood blue chiffon. I'd been told by the designer the blue matched my eyes.

But if Zip thought so, he was too reserved to say.

"Gee, Barbara," he said shyly, "since I met you, being stationed in New York City has been so much fun."

"For me, too, Zip," I murmured.

"It's great spending all this time together. I really feel I'm getting to know you."

"That's great, Zip. I'm glad." I took a deep breath, then proceeded with the words I'd been rehearsing all day. "But unfortunately, I'm getting to know you, too. And I'm afraid the more I know you, the more I like you. Why, yesterday I even found myself thinking about you when I was trying to work."

Zip looked at me in surprise. "Is that so bad?"

I nodded sadly. "It's against everything I stand for. I won't let myself be distracted by a man, Zip." I gazed at his face, his features so handsome in the moonlight. I was wavering, but I had to stick to my plans. "I have to warn you, if I start to really care about you, any kind of relationship will be out of the question."

Zip stared at me with big puppy-dog eyes. "Oh, no! Don't say that, Barbara! Couldn't you keep from caring about me for just a little while longer until I care for you just a little bit more?"

I sighed, rather smitten by his logic. "I'll try."

He scooched a fraction of an inch closer. "How about a kiss?" he whispered.

"Please."

I closed my eyes, waiting in anticipation for the kiss I'd been dreaming of for weeks.

Then I felt Zip slip something into my hand.

I opened my eyes and looked down.

The moonlight glinted off the silver wrapper of a single Hershey's Kiss.

Disappointed, but hanging in there, I unwrapped the Kiss and popped it into my mouth.

"I appreciate your patience," Zip said shyly. "Any other girl in this city would have made me feel like a hick."

Sucking on the chocolate, I rested my head on his

shoulder . . . and watched as Zip tossed his homemade fishing pole back into the lake in Central Park.

At least I had someone I found desirable to cuddle with. And we did have fun together. But the queen of sex à la carte was still going hungry.

What was I doing wrong?

CATCHER

When Peter called me at the office from his apartment and said it was an emergency, I changed my shirt and ran right over. He answered the door in an apron and stuck a soup ladle in my face.

"Quick! Taste my sauce. Too tart?"

I was stunned. "This is your big emergency?"

Peter turned and raced to the kitchen. I hurried after him.

"Yes!" Peter exclaimed. "I invited Vikki to dinner, and it has to be perfect so she'll find me irresistible and I can make my big move."

Whew. "You should've made your big move three weeks ago, Mac. I keep telling you, that's these *Down with Love* girls' claim to fame—one date, no waiting."

"Well, these *Down with Love* girls may be used to having sex the way a man does, but I'm not." He handed me the ladle. "Too sweet?"

I handed it back without tasting. "To each his own."

Peter opened a pot on the stove and stirred.

"So, I guess you and Novak have been *very* 'down with

102

love.' I mean, you've had, what, twenty-nine dates in twenty-three days."

"Yeah, only I'm trying to get her to not want to have sex with me, and these days you have to really play your cards right to get a girl to say no."

Peter gave me a sidelong glance. "Or maybe you just like spending time with her. Maybe the necessity of all this chastity and monogamy has made you realize that Barbara Novak is your ideal potential lover."

He was dreaming. "Come back to Earth, buddy boy. Your cake's burning."

Peter grabbed his oven mitts and hurried to the oven to rescue the soufflé. I watched him thoughtfully.

I was having a crazy thought. It seemed almost impossible to imagine, but maybe—just maybe—I could actually learn something from Peter. About women.

"This is how a guy like you does it, huh?"

Peter put the soufflé on a trivet. "No. I don't do it. But if I did do it, I'd do what I'm doing. Which reminds me of something I didn't do. I have to call Vikki and give her my address."

"I've got a better idea," I said. "Invite Vikki to my place. Make like it's yours. You know where I keep the spare key."

A sly grin spread across Peter's face. "You'd let me use the secret key for your girlfriends?"

"Somebody might as well use it. It's been collecting dust ever since Novak hit the bestseller list."

"But I invited Vikki to a home-cooked meal," Peter said, worried.

"Trust me. Ten minutes in my place, and you'll both forget all about dinner."

Peter's grin changed to nervous. "Ten minutes?"

I nodded. "Ten minutes."

Barbara

I was sunbathing on my deck in an itsy-bitsy teenie-weenie yellow polka-dot bikini, with matching sun hat and Jacqueline Kennedy–style sunglasses, that I'd purchased on one of my shopping excursions to Bloomingdale's. When I tried on the bikini, I made a point of coming out of the dressing room to give Zip a little preview and ask his opinion.

But after taking one long look at my body, he hustled me back into the dressing room, then excused himself and hurried outside to buy a newspaper and wait. I wasn't sure whether to take that as a compliment or not.

Now I was working on my tan, and trying to work on ideas for my next book. But Zip Martin kept getting in the way.

Not literally—don't I wish.

But in my mind. The situation was definitely giving me ideas. But not the kind I needed.

The phone rang, and I slipped on my heels to dash in and answer it.

"Hello?"

"Hello, Barbara. It's Zip."

I tingled all over at the sound of his voice. Especially when I heard the sound of water running in the background. Gosh, he was probably just stepping out of the shower, all deliciously clean and smelling like an Irish spring, the water droplets glistening in his thick dark hair, on his smooth heated skin.

"Hello, Zip," I said warmly. I imagined him wrapping his lean hips in a lush terry-cloth towel emblazoned with a Z—like the mark of Zorro.

When you visit Disneyland, they tell you in the Tomorrow Land that one day we'll have telephones with TV-like screens.

But right now I was doing just fine without one.

"I was wondering," he asked in a deep, almost pained voice, "if I could ask you to do me a very special favor."

I dropped by sunglasses and went down on the floor to retrieve them. As I stayed there on my knees, I heard the unmistakable sound of thick-piled terry cloth buffing firm tanned skin. The accompanying vision was quite disturbing. I began to blow on my sunglasses, then swallowed, thinking I was changing my mind about the picture phone. "Sure, Zip," I responded like a woman in you-know-what. "*Anything.*" And I meant it.

"I know we planned to go out," he began.

Oh, no! Was he breaking our date—right when I needed one most?

"But I thought it might be fun to stay in," he drawled.

In was good. A list of things we could do began to form in my mind.

There were new noises over the phone, and I strained to identify them.

Hmm, it sounded as if he'd switched to doing sit-ups.

Even in my bikini, I was beginning to feel a bit warm and overdressed.

"I'm in the mood . . ." he said, grunting with exertion.

Uh-huh. So was I. My eyes drifted closed . . .

". . . for a home-cooked meal."

GONG! His words were like an ice-cold piña colada spilled down my heaving cleavage. "Major Martin," I announced firmly, "I know you haven't read my book, but I have no desire to stay cooped up in the kitchen slaving over a hot stove and a sink full of dirty dishes."

To calm myself down, I leaned back and extended like a waterfall into one of my favorite stretches, a full gymnastic backbend—a move that's very good for soothing tensions, flattening the tummy, and keeping the hips sex-à-la-carte limber.

"Oh, no, Barbara! You misunderstood," Zip rushed to explain. "When I said a home-cooked meal, I meant at *my* place." His voice lowered a notch. "I meant *I* wanted to serve *you.*"

As my hands touched the floor at the zenith of my extended position, I let the full meaning of his suggestion completely fill me with pleasure.

"Oh, Zip!" I moaned, my muscles trembling. "No man has ever done this for me before! How thoughtful . . . and considerate . . ." Thanks to an extremely flexible phone cord, I managed to find my way to the conversation area of my sunken living room and collapse on the couch, feeling myself open completely to this astounding and unpredictable man.

"So," he asked, his breath coming in measured pants, as if he'd switched to doing push-ups, "you'd like to come?"

"Yes . . . yes . . . yes!" I cried.

"I can't wait!" he exclaimed, then groaned, sounding as if he had collapsed onto his back on the floor.

I lay there on the couch in utter bliss for a moment, gazing out my floor-to-ceiling windows at the Technicolor blue sky, enjoying the afterglow of social intercourse via Princess phone with the most desirable man I'd ever met. I pictured him lying beside me, happy and content.

How I longed to try out similar positions with him—in the same apartment.

Neither of us spoke for a moment, and then Zip sighed and politely gave me his address. "Seventy-third and Park."

Lazily I stretched out one leg and wrote the address in the air with one pointed, manicured toe.

Mmm. Another good way to tone those inner thighs.

"And Barbara . . . ?" Zip murmured.

"Yes, Zip?" I sighed dreamily.

"Thank you for being so flexible."

"No, Zip," I murmured. "Thank *you*."

I blew him a kiss he couldn't hear or see, then waited for him to be the first one to hang up.

Just before he broke the connection, I heard the unmistakable sound of a fine engraved metal lighter flicking open just as I was reaching for my own post-heart-to-heart cigarette.

I smiled as I inhaled a deep satisfying drag.

I guess the call was as good for him as it was for me.

Barbara

That night I showed up at Zip's apartment, and let me tell you, I'd never been more surprised in my life.

It was like *Good Housekeeping* and *Cosmopolitan* all rolled into one.

First of all, he answered the door with a frilly apron tied around his trim hips, and didn't seem to care a bit what it might do to his masculine image.

Then he led me into his apartment, which was absolutely beautiful, with a very modern decor—elegant and yet decidedly masculine. Books, paintings, antiques, a piano . . . Had he rented the place furnished, I wondered, or were these things his own personal touch?

Either way he was definitely at home here.

And on top of everything the place was spotless. I didn't know if he had a maid, but if he did, I wanted her number.

Dinner was ready, so he immediately led me to the dining table and held out my chair for me.

I sat down and gazed at the table in amazement. White tablecloth, beautiful place settings, candles, flowers . . . a table that would put most housewives to shame.

It was a delightful surprise.

Some men might have come across, well, rather sissy in such a setting.

But not this man.

The contrast of feminine skills, even the frilly apron tied around his hips, only served to heighten my awareness of his masculine appeal.

"Oh, Zip, everything looks wonderful!" I gushed, definitely including him in the "everything."

With a smile, he whipped the napkin from the table and smoothed it across my lap.

I swallowed. "I have a funny feeling you've done quite a bit of 'entertaining for two' here."

Zip shook his head. "I can honestly say, until you, I haven't done any 'entertaining for two' here at all."

"You're certainly not the average astronaut," I commented.

I felt a shiver as he served me from behind, his cheek so close to mine as he poured the wine, filling my glass.

"I get so tired of all that freeze-dried food," he murmured in my ear. "After a steady diet of pellet steaks and potato tablets, you yearn for something *hot* to sink your teeth into."

Tell me about it. I was ravenous—and for far more than his home-cooked pot roast. All I had to do was turn my head, and his lips would be touching mine.

I could almost taste his kisses.

But before I could move, the moment slipped away and he slid into his seat across the table from me. In my current state, the distance seemed like miles.

His eyes never left mine as he lifted a lid from a chafing dish of vegetables, hot from the stove. I licked my lips as I gazed at him through the steam.

I hoped he wasn't a mirage.

"Well, you've whetted my appetite," I murmured, "and it's not just your cooking." I glanced around his apartment. "You are so well rounded. Your collection of art and antiques and your library. You've made a real home here."

"Well," Zip said modestly, "Earth is still my favorite planet."

"No, I meant here in New York," I said. "Most bachelors in this city are only interested in an apartment that comes fully loaded with every gadget and contraption man has invented to snare a woman!"

For some reason, he choked a bit on his wine at that. But then he recovered and offered me a second helping of mashed potatoes.

I couldn't wait for dessert.

CATCHER

Even with every gadget and contraption man has invented at his disposal, Peter was still helpless. I couldn't have imagined what he later told me was happening while Barbara and I were at his place. It all started when he lost the cocktail bar.

Most gentlemen, myself included, keep their *affaires de coeur* confidential. Kiss-and-tell went out with show-and-tell.

But Peter was one of those poor slobs who just had to spill his guts about everything. Here's what he said happened.

Vikki sat on the couch, smoking, while Peter fumbled along the mirrored wall above the master control panel, looking for a secret button.

"I don't understand this, Peter," Vikki said. "How does a person 'lose' his built-in bar?"

Peter scowled at the panel of buttons. There aren't that many. Half a dozen. What was the problem? "I swear," he told her, "it was right here a minute ago."

So he pushed the one labeled *C*, thinking it might stand

for "cocktails," but of course it's just button C, the third one from the left after buttons A and B. Anyway, it caused the seat of the couch Vikki was on to suddenly shoot out from the wall, throwing her onto the floor and then running over her as it elongated to bed size.

Peter hadn't noticed. He tried *B* for "bar," and that one, coincidentally, worked. Personally I'm surprised Peter didn't gravitate immediately to *A*, the first letter in another name for *donkey*.

"Hey! I found it!" Peter said, looking around for his date. "Vikki? Where are you?"

"I don't know!" came her muffled voice.

Peter spotted a plume of cigarette smoke rising from under the couch. He choked back the urge to cry out for help, then dropped to his knees and rescued Vikki on his own.

"Peter," Vikki gasped as she wriggled out, "your couch was all over me like some animal! Who knew you were so dangerous!"

"I'm sorry, I'm sorry," Peter apologized profusely. "I know I seem a little disoriented. I guess I tasted too much sherry while I was cooking."

"You cooked for me?" Vikki exclaimed. "No man has ever done that for me before! I'm famished!"

Peter winced. "Actually, I didn't cook here—at my apartment—for us. I cooked at Catch's apartment." He was cornered now. Why would he be cooking at Catch's? "For . . . Catch."

"Oh."

"But you've only been here a minute," he reminded her, sauntering to the bar, then showing her my martini glasses and parroting something I'd said to him that was never intended for Vikki. "Let's make it ten and see if we forget about dinner."

He didn't report her reaction to that—probably because he was too nervous to notice it.

Then Peter poured gin while Vikki looked at the pictures on my walls.

"Are these your parents?" she asked about one.

Peter glanced up and then went back to the cocktails, preoccupied with the measurement of vermouth. "No. Those are Catch's parents."

Vikki found that odd, of course. "Why do you have a picture of Catch's parents?"

Peter woke up finally and tried to change the subject. "Let's listen to some music!" he babbled, and punched a button on the console.

An LP dropped from the changer arm onto the turntable—and the loudest section of the *1812* Overture blasted across the room.

So he hit another button.

And the lights went out.

Frantic, he started wildly pounding the console like a punching bag. The record speed shot to 45, then 78. The lights flashed on and off. The couch flipped back and forth, in and out of the wall. When Peter switched to two hands on the console, records flew out of the stereo like UFOs.

Peter and Vikki, ducking the saucers, yelled back and forth over the chaos.

"I'm sorry about this, Vikki," Peter whimpered apologetically. "I know I promised you a romantic, intimate evening."

"Maybe we should try somewhere more quiet," Vikki hollered, "like the Oyster Bar at Grand Central Station!"

"Good idea!" Peter shouted. "I can't do *this* for eight more minutes! Let's go eat!"

He grabbed her by the hand and they ran out the door.

I'll always remember it as the one time I got an actual warning letter from my cleaning lady.

Barbara

W e'd left the table in ruins—candles guttering in their silver holders, the remains of the meal spread across the table like a scene from the movie version of *Tom Jones*.

And now Zip was whispering in my ear.

"How's that?" he murmured. "You tell me when it's good for you. Put your hand on it and guide me until I've got it on the right spot."

"Almost . . . almost . . . Oh, Zip!" I gushed. "I've done this a lot before, of course, but never with such a powerful instrument."

Okay, dear reader, calm down. Pour yourself a Tab on ice.

If I'm doing a tell-all confessional here, I guess the only honest thing to do is to tell all.

The dialogue above? Oh, sure, I could type it up and start a whole new line of Barbara Novak books—sexually explicit romance novels. (Not that any publisher could ever get away with printing anything like that!)

But the truth is: the image in your mind of what we were doing . . . is pure fiction.

After dinner Zip and I had strolled out onto his fabulous balcony. All of Manhattan lay twinkling before us like a jewelry store of multicolored gems spilled across a magic carpet of black velvet.

Above us the full moon seemed close enough to touch.

It was all wonderfully romantic.

But I suppose it's not a surprise that astronauts look at the moon and stars in a slightly different way than the rest of us. Zip had this powerful state-of-the-art telescope set up on his balcony, and he was showing me how to find the moon.

Zip had one arm around me, the other covering my hand and guiding the focus. And our cheeks were nearly, *nearly* touching.

"That's it!" I exclaimed, squinting through the telescope as the craters of the moon came into focus. "It's perfectly clear. Oh, Zip! I've never seen anything so beautiful in all my life!"

"Neither have I."

I chuckled. "But you're not even looking through the telescope."

"I know," Zip breathed.

Confused, I turned from the telescope and our eyes locked.

He'd been staring at me. Was he saying I was beautiful?

I couldn't move. I was on fire.

The many positions of the astrological sex chart in the

addendum to my book suddenly flashed through my mind, and like a woman opening a new box of chocolates, I felt an overwhelming desire to take a bite out of each one.

But I didn't. I put the lid back on.

Okay, stop shrieking for a moment and I'll tell you why the h— not.

Because a metaphorical lightning bolt suddenly illuminated my heart the way a real bolt of lightning enables you to see everything around you for a quick instant on a dark, hot summer night.

I realized what I was feeling was more than pure lust. Far more. And it scared the hell out of me.

Sex was supposed to be a game—a little light entertainment between two equal adults, a break from the labor of two careers.

But once again I'd found myself in a situation where I cared too much for a man who didn't care enough.

A flat-out betrayal of *Down with Love* rules.

Taking a deep, shuddering breath, I untangled myself and strode quickly to the coffee table, where moments ago we'd indulged in dessert. "This chocolate soufflé is delicious," I said brightly as I shoveled a hunk into my mouth. "You've really outdone yourself."

"Well," Zip said huskily, following me into the living room, "I wanted the perfect end to the perfect evening."

I turned. Our eyes locked. Time stood still.

Oh, darn!

My knees went weak, and I sank to the couch.

Zip sat down beside me. And then he whispered those words I'd been longing to hear. Words that might make it all work out.

"I've never been more ready to go to bed."

GONG! That little bell went off in my head again.

Forget what I said before. He was ready. I was more than ready. Two equally matched opponents in the war between the sexes.

I'd sort out the particulars in the morning.

"I'm so glad you feel that way, Zip," I breathed, my eyes glistening with tears of joy as my spoon fell noisily into the glass soufflé dish. "You know I feel the same way."

"Well, then," he drawled, "let's get to bed."

Ding! Ding! Ding! The little bell in my head had turned into a three-alarm fire. Trembling with excitement, I reached out to take his hand.

His eyes bored into mine. I leaned forward for his kiss. And then he murmured in his sexiest voice, "I'll call you a taxi."

BOING! My eyes crossed, and my head filled with the sound of rush-hour traffic screeching to a halt. "Taxi?" I repeated like an idiot.

Zip stared at me, a puzzled frown doing nothing to mar his handsome features.

And then I saw a light come on in his brain.

"Oh!" His eyes popped open. "When I said 'bed,' you thought I meant . . . *bed*!" He stumbled up from the couch like a little boy caught with his hand in the cookie jar. "I'm sorry, Barbara! But . . . gosh . . . this is only the first time you've been to my home, and where I come from—"

I rose to my feet and held up my hand. "It's all right, Zip. It's better this way." I straightened my skirt, patted my hair, and then smiled. "Let's just say good night. And"—I held out my hand—"good-bye."

"Good-bye?!" Zip exclaimed. "You mean, for good?"

"I'm afraid so, Zip. I'm beginning to feel . . . well, I'm beginning to *feel*!"

He moved to block the door. "Couldn't you give me just one more chance?" he begged.

"I'd like to, Zip," I said, regaining my *Down with Love* resolve. "Really, I would. But the fact that I'd *like* to give you another chance is the very reason why I absolutely must not—"

He suddenly took my face in his hands and kissed me— hard, passionately, and with tremendous skill.

The astronaut took me straight to the moon.

When we pulled apart, I could only stare at him, dazed. The little ding-dong bell in my head had turned into a whole town of church bells ringing as madly as a Dickens Christmas morning.

"Okay, then . . ." I said when I managed to catch my

breath. "One more chance . . . And . . . I'll just take the rest of that *chocolate* soufflé to go."

I scooped up my coat and the glass dessert dish, and like a drunk trying to negotiate a straight line for a cop, I wobbled, weak-kneed, to the door and let myself out.

CATCHER

Barbara left and closed the door behind her, and I still hadn't moved since she kissed me. Finally I did.

I crossed to the table and removed the champagne bottle from the ice bucket, then carried the bucket outside on the balcony. Then I raised it, took a deep breath, and gave myself what I really needed.

An ice-cold shower.

Back in control, I decided to return to my apartment and see what I could salvage of the night.

On the elevator ride to my place I took off my Zip Martin glasses and wondered what was happening to me. Whatever it was, the only remedy I knew would be a scotch on the rocks in the sanctity of my own little corner of the world—in my own little bachelor pad. When the doors opened I heard the muffled sound of a hot little jazz number I easily recognized, because I happened to own a copy of the record. That copy happened to be the one I was hearing. In my own little bachelor pad.

I went to the door, turned the key in the lock, and opened it. It scared me at first when smoke poured out—

but quickly I could see the place wasn't on fire. It was just that my apartment was full of beatniks and they were having a party.

MY APARTMENT IS FULL OF BEATNIKS AND THEY'RE HAVING A PARTY! my mind screamed.

"Excuse me," I demanded of a nearby representative of the counterculture. "Is Peter MacMannus here?"

"You mean the Wizard?" Jack Kerouac Jr. replied. He pointed across the room. "He's over there."

I spotted the man he was talking about and recognized him as Peter. Not at first. It took me a few seconds. The man I was looking at was wearing a beret and beads, and was barefoot, sitting Indian style on the bar. He kept disappearing and reappearing as the mirrored wall opened and closed.

I strode over to him and hit the button that stopped the bar from moving, keeping my barely recognizable friend visible in the present realm. "Peter?" I said.

He bobbed his head at me. "You rang?"

"No, Maynard. I used my key. How did everybody else get in?"

Peter smiled dreamily. "I took Vikki down to the Village for a demitasse. Crazy! Then the coffeehouse got raided, so I moved the scene uptown. You dig, daddy-o?"

I looked across the room and spotted a beatnik girl behind raccoon-style eyeliner, wearing a beret, boots, and nothing else in between except for a Lady Godiva hairstyle. And she was headed straight for me. My outlook toward the party changed dramatically.

"I *do* dig," I assured Peter. "After being grounded for twenty-four days, this astronaut is ready to blast off."

I hit a button and made Peter disappear again. I wasn't in the mood to share. Especially this morsel.

I smiled as she approached me, admiring the way her hair kept her decent, barely, and wondering where I'd stored my desk fan.

"Ask me why I mourn," the beatnik girl said mournfully.

"Why do you mourn, baby?" I said, playing along.

"I mourn because you're shrouded in the suit and tie that Madison Avenue will bury you in alive," she said.

I liked the way she thought—I definitely had a problem. But another way of looking at a problem is to see it as an opportunity. "If it'll cheer you up," I said, "you can help me out of it."

Lady G. smiled and took me by my tie. I followed her like Rin Tin Tin, panting. I was ready for my walk around the block. Or the bedroom.

She chose to take me to the latter.

Barbara

I was a drowning woman, sinking fast.

But not long after I made it home to my apartment, Vikki called and tossed me a life preserver. I could barely hear her over the noise in the background.

It sounded like she was having a party.

She was, she told me. Sort of . . . Then someone turned the music up and I could barely hear what she said.

I still didn't quite understand, but she said I'd get hip to the scene as soon as I arrived. "Think beatnik!" she shouted, hollered the address, then hung up.

Hip to the scene? I stared at the receiver. It sounded like some wild, out-of-control beatnik party.

I grinned. It was exactly what I needed.

I changed clothes in record time and caught a cab to the address she'd given me—a high-rise apartment building in a very good neighborhood. Not your usual bohemian scene.

Once I got off the elevator, it was easy to find the party. All I had to do was follow the sound of jazz drifting down the hall like the aroma of some exotic soup. That and the plumes of smoke.

I knocked politely a couple of times. Rang the bell. But it soon became obvious that no one could hear me over the noise of the party.

I didn't normally walk right into people's private abodes, but I was Barbara Novak, queen of the bestsellers. And I had been invited after all.

Plus, I'd had such a wonderful, painful, *confusing* evening with Zip Martin; I needed a wild party to barge into.

So I cautiously opened the door and peeked inside.

It was my first beatnik party, and I hoped that in my black velvet Capri pants and black turtleneck, topped with a yellow brocade pea coat and matching brocade beret, finished off with black velvet high heels—all by Chanel—I'd blend in with the crowd.

I squeezed in and just managed to shut the door behind me. *Blend in!?* Gosh, the apartment was so jammed, I feared we'd all be blended into a beatnik puree before the night was through.

I looked around for a familiar face and at last spotted Vikki coming out of the kitchen—carrying a tray of coffee. I tsked. Senior editor at Banner House Publishing and she was still serving up the joe. I guess old habits die hard.

"Hi!" I called out over the noise, waving as she made her way through the gyrating crowd without spilling a drop. "So, this is a beatnik party."

"Isn't it a gas?" she shouted back.

I nodded. "I'm so glad you called," I yelled. "After the date I had tonight, I really didn't want to be alone."

"You won't need an astronaut to find a date in here," Vikki said with a wink. "Everyone's in orbit!"

A beatnik boy walked by. On his hands. Vikki held out her tray toward his bare feet. "Coffee?"

The boy paused. Vikki obliged by carefully balancing a cup and saucer of steaming java on the sole of his foot. I watched in amazement as he walked away through the crowd without a spill.

You're definitely walking on the wild side tonight, I told myself.

"Don't use the sugar cubes," Vikki warned with a wink, "or you'll be in orbit, too."

"Thanks," I said. "Should I introduce myself to the host, or is that too 'establishment'?"

"Oh! You know the host," Vikki replied. "This is Peter's place."

Peter? Peter *MacMannus*? I looked around at the apartment. Odd . . . Of course, I didn't know Peter that well, but he seemed such a nice, quiet, dignified kind of man—a man whose apartment would be filled with books, paintings, antiques, a piano . . . more like Zip Martin's place than this jazzy flat.

This place seemed more like a swinging bachelor pad designed to seduce women.

I shrugged. You couldn't tell a book by its cover, nor a

man by the cut of his suit. And as I advised my readers in chapter thirteen of *Down with Love*, no matter how well you thought you knew a man, no matter how well you trusted him, he was probably harboring at least one deep dark secret that would knock your stockings off if you ever found out.

I guess there was more to Peter MacMannus than met the eye.

Then a horrible thought occurred to me. If this was Peter's place, Peter's party, wouldn't his friends and staff be invited, too?

I clutched at Vikki's sleeve and glanced around. "Catcher Block isn't going to be here, is he?" I asked.

"Not to worry!" Vikki replied. "Everyone here is a complete stranger. Coffee?" she said to two beatniks who were snapping their fingers as they bebopped by.

But something was still bothering me. "Vikki, I don't understand," I said as we twisted between a couple of twisters. "How did your 'intimate date' turn into a party?"

"Oh, that's Peter," she said with a slightly forced smile. "He always wants to show me off."

But she couldn't fool me. I could read her like a book. Gosh, I'd written the book. "What about what *you* want?" I asked her. "You can't expect a man to read your mind. You have to tell a man exactly what you want and how you want it."

Vikki studied my face, mulling over my words, and I

could see the age-old struggles going on behind her Max Factor eyeliner and mascara.

Then those eyes caught fire, and she set her serving tray firmly aside. "You're right, Barbara," she said with determination. "And when I get it, I want you right there behind me."

Oh! I thought, flustered. I wasn't sure I was *that* forward thinking. Had this wild party gone to her head?

"You know, when I ask Theodore Banner to give me the same authority as the other senior editors," Vikki clarified.

"Oh," I said. "*Ohhhh.*" Now that I had *that* straightened out, I felt an overwhelming sense of pride wash over me. A new woman was being born this very moment, right before my eyes, and I had personally handled the forceps. But my work, like an obstetrician's, was done. "Oh, Vikki!" I told her. "You don't need *me* there! And you're smart to go straight to the top dog. But don't *ask. Demand* equal authority. And while you're at it, equal *pay!*"

"Equal *pay?*" Vikki guffawed. "Oh, Barbara, you slay me! Now, enough shoptalk. This is a party! We're here to have fun. Go throw your coat on the bed and join the bash."

She squeezed my hand, then went off to serve coffee with a completely new attitude. I wiggled out of my brocade jacket as I squeezed my way through the jostling, dancing mass of humanity.

Down the hall I found the bedroom and opened the door.

The room was dark, too dark to see the bed. Groping along the wall, I found the switch and flicked on the lights—

And instantly realized there was something else on the bed besides coats and purses. Something writhing in passion. A man and a girl.

"Oh!" I exclaimed, and instantly covered my eyes. "Excuse me!" I blindly tossed my coat in the general direction of the bed and sang out, "Catch!"

"Yes?"

Huh?

That voice. That deep, sexy, very masculine voice. It sounded awfully familiar . . .

Don't look, I told myself, but of course I did. I peeked through my fingers—and couldn't believe my eyes.

Of all the bedrooms at all the parties in Manhattan, I had to walk into this one. Ignorance would have been bliss.

But it was too late. I recognized the man on the bed, even without his glasses. But I guess he didn't need them for this job. "Zip!" I exclaimed.

Jerking upright, he did.

Zip! . . . Such a tiny everyday sound.

But that one tiny sound turned my stomach. And turned my world upside down.

"But I just got him *un*-zipped!" moaned the beatnik girl who lay beneath him.

I shuddered with . . . what? Anger, humiliation, betrayal—and a thousand other emotions that I'd invited into my own heart the day I let myself have feelings for this man.

"Well," I replied hotly, "don't let me interrupt you." I grabbed my brocade jacket, dodged Zip's outreached hand, and marched away from the scene of the crime as quickly as my black velvet heels would take me.

"Barbara, wait!" I heard him call out behind me. But I didn't even look back.

I was angry—darned straight, I was! But mostly I was angry with myself. I'd fought my way to the top of the bestseller list by preaching new rules for this insane game of sex and love. But I'd broken my strictest rule:

Give your body, but never, ever your heart.

If I felt betrayed, it was I who had betrayed my own heart.

I fought my way through the writhing, dancing mob like a salmon swimming upstream. I didn't even look for Vikki to tell her good-bye. I just knew I had to get out of there—now!

I finally stumbled into the hallway, then fled toward the sheltering privacy of the elevator.

"Barbara!" I heard Zip shout.

I couldn't believe he'd had the nerve to follow me.

I poked and poked at the down button, begging it to hurry.

Ding! At last the elevator arrived and the doors whooshed open. I dashed inside, jabbing *L* for "lobby." Thank goodness the doors were closing—

Then Zip stuck his hand in to hold the doors. "Please," he begged. "I can explain."

I should have ignored him. I should have held my tongue. But I was too angry. "You don't have to explain to me," I said curtly. "You said you were ready for bed. I'm glad you ran into someone you care enough for to take to bed with you. Although if you ask me, she's the one who should have gotten dinner out of it."

"It's not like that!" he insisted. "I don't even know her!"

"Oh, really?!" I rolled my eyes. As if that made it better!

"I mean, I didn't know what I was doing," he clarified.

I glanced down. "And yet her hat's off to you anyway."

He stared down at himself and had the decency to look embarrassed.

The beatnik girl's beret was stuck in his quickly zipped-up zipper.

With a sigh, he stood back, and the elevator doors closed.

The elevator ride seemed endless, but at last it hit bottom, and I literally flew through the lobby.

"Good night, miss," the doorman called politely as he held the door.

Ding! I heard another elevator open behind me.

The sound of a well-heeled man clicked across the polished linoleum floor. "Good night, Major Martin!" I heard the doorman say.

Ignore him. Pretend he doesn't exist, I told myself as I stepped into the street to hail a cab.

But then I felt his hand on my arm, and it wasn't static electricity I felt.

Calling myself every kind of fool, I turned around to listen to what he had to say.

CATCHER

Yes. The elevator touched down in the nick of time. Barbara was just heading out the door. "Good night, Major Martin!" I heard the doorman say as I ran into the street where she was searching for a cab.

I called her name, and she turned around. If looks could kill . . . She wasn't going to make this easy.

"Barbara," I pleaded. "You've got to believe me. I didn't know what was happening. The minute I got here, that girl filled my pipe with some tobacco she bought in San Francisco, and from then on, everything went hooey!"

She turned to me with a look of concern, and studied my face. I was about to find out once and for all just how good a liar I was.

"Zip! You mean she drugged you?"

Answer: I was good. I forced myself not to smile.

I nodded forlornly. "All the way into that bedroom!" I was very good.

"Oh, Zip!" she said, softening. "You should have known better than to smoke someone else's tobacco at a party like that— Wait a minute. What exactly were you doing at a party like that? You don't like parties."

"I had no idea there was going to be a party there," I said, practically believing every word I said. "I got a call after you left to come to this publisher guy's apartment to meet some journalist who wants to do a cover story on my NASA top secret project. Some guy named Snitch . . . or Snatch . . ."

"Catch? Catcher Block?"

I frowned and looked groggy from that stuff that girl put in my pipe. "Maybe. So I rush over here and the guy never shows up."

She was steamed. "Definitely Catcher Block!"

"Isn't that *rude*?" I said, making the vowel sounds drag on forever.

"It's more than rude, Zip. Don't you see? You were set up! That marijuana girl was a plant!"

"No!" I said in disbelief. Disbelief that Barbara was not only believing my lies—she was embellishing them for me. It was too good to be true!

"Yes! Catcher Block had you invited here under false pretenses so he could do one of his famous exposés on how NASA's top secret New York project is just one big drug-infested beatnik shindig!"

"Oh! That's *low*!" I said, egging her on.

"*That's* Catcher Block! *That's* how he operates! He tricks people into doing things completely out of character, and the people don't even know they're being tricked. Makes you wonder if he's ever written an honest word in his life."

Ouch. "Well, now hold on—" I said. I knew she was upset, but saying Catcher Block couldn't write—that was going a little far.

"He's nothing more than an amoral insidious sneak!" Barbara said.

Double ouch. This me-bashing was going a little too far.

"Come on, Barbara," I said. "He must be a little more than that. After all, he won the Pulitzer Prize."

She looked shocked. "Are you defending him?"

Now I was the one getting upset. "He doesn't need to be defended. A man doesn't win the Pulitzer Prize for being an insidious sneak. Ever think of that?"

Barbara peered at me strangely. "Zip, why do you care what I think about Catcher Block?"

"I don't!" I said loudly. Too loudly. *Get ahold of yourself*, I thought. *Or you'll blow the whole deal.* "I mean, I don't," I repeated. Quick, quick! How to play this? Ah! I know. I smiled inwardly at my own genius and whined, "I guess I just feel like such an easily tricked hick! And then you went and made the trick seem so obvious—"

"Zip," Barbara cooed, "I didn't mean to make you feel bad."

"And I didn't mean to make you feel mad," I moaned apologetically. We were back on track.

"This is terrible," Barbara said with a soft chuckle, swaying toward me slightly. "We're behaving like two people in love."

Our eyes locked.

I wondered if I looked as scared as she did.

"Which means," Barbara said, all business again, "this argument was the final straw, Zip. This has to be the end."

She extended her hand for me to shake.

A handshake!

Damn!

Come on, Catcher—work that rod! Don't let this one get away!

"Or . . . just the beginning!" I said, suddenly beaming. "Holy cow! This argument has made me realize I must really care about you! I finally care enough to get to know you better!"

I took her in my arms and squeezed her tight.

Barbara resisted. "How much better?" she asked warily.

"All the way better!" I said huskily.

"Really?" she whispered.

"Yes!" I took her face in my hands. I stared into her beautiful eyes. "I'm sorry to have to say this, Barbara, but—I love you!"

I felt her soften like butter in my arms, felt her tremble like a leaf.

Or was that me?

"Well"—she sighed—"I have no rules against *men* falling in love."

Bingo! "So there's still time for us?" I asked hopefully. "I mean, you're still not in love with me. Right?"

"Yes . . ."

"So I could make love to you—heartfelt, passionate, worshiping, adoring love—and you could still have meaningless sex with me. Right?"

"Yes . . ."

"Then we're still on for tomorrow night?"

She was looking at me for all the world like a woman in love. "Yes! Oh, yes!"

We embraced, and I felt an immense wave of relief wash over me. I guess the doorman saw it, too, because he gave me a salute. I winked and gave him a thumbs-up behind Barbara's back.

Barbara

The next day turned out to be a pivotal moment in all our lives.

I wasn't there at that fateful meeting at Banner House. And Vikki didn't arrive till late.

But Theodore Banner's secretary was keeping the minutes, and she passed them to Gladys, who shared them with Vikki and me.

Here's what happened.

Apparently T.B. had ordered an emergency staff meeting, and accidentally on purpose neglected to inform his senior *female* editor.

He stood in his favorite spot, right beneath the oil painting of himself, and admonished his men like a general who was disappointed in his troops.

"That pink book is ruining my life!" he shouted. "The woman acts like she has a mind of her own! She refuses my advances! This goes straight to the sanctity of our most sacred institution!"

J.B. nodded gravely. "All our wives are giving us trouble."

"I'm not talking about my wife!" Banner bellowed. "I'm talking about my mistress!"

His staff nodded sympathetically, for once thankful they had only one woman in their lives.

He glared at his men and pounded the mahogany table. "I want that Vikki Hiller fired!"

His order delivered, he stormed out into the reception area. The men followed on his heels.

"We can't fire her now, T.B.," E.G. argued. "How would it look? She's the most celebrated editor in the business."

"You're my creative team," Banner growled. "*Create* a reason to get rid of her! Or I'll create a new creative team!"

He stomped off to his office and slammed the door.

His men huddled in silence, clearly shaken.

Ding! Just then the elevator doors opened, and who should appear but Vikki Hiller herself, smiling, confident, upbeat, never breaking her stride as she strutted past the men and headed straight to Banner's office.

"Good morning, gentlemen." She paused to greet them. "And do you know why it's good? Because this is the morning I tell Theodore Banner that my *fellow* senior editors are going to treat me like more than just a titular senior editor or I *quit*!"

With a firm nod of her head, she marched into Banner's office and shut the door firmly behind her.

They listened. But they couldn't hear a thing.

Which didn't really matter anyway.

Their grins returned and they all sauntered back to their offices.

They wouldn't have to figure out a way to get rid of the annoying Vikki Hiller.

She'd done their job for them.

✳

Later that day Vikki lay on my couch as I poured her another cup of coffee. A cardboard carton on the floor held all her personal belongings from her job.

I couldn't believe she'd been fired. Who fired an editor responsible for an international bestseller?

"I should have known the top dog would be a rat," Vikki complained bitterly. "He's a man. I hate men. For as man-crazy as I've been my whole life, I sure can't stand them." She sighed in resignation. "I think I'll just get married."

"You're just upset," I reassured her. "You'll find another job."

"I don't want another job!" she exclaimed. "Another building full of men who will all hate me until I hate them! I've had it! I'm sorry, Barbara, but I don't want to be a *Down with Love* girl anymore. I give up. I give in. I just want to be Mrs. Peter MacMannus."

"Really?"

"At least then there would be one man I could tell what to do. Anyway, there, I said it. So if you want me to also resign as your friend, I'll understand."

Poor girl. She really was distraught. I took her hand in mine. "Oh, Vikki. I couldn't accept your resignation now when I need a friend more than ever. You see, I have a confession to make, too."

I glanced around. Like a cold war spy at the Pentagon, I tiptoed to the door and locked it. Then locked my patio door, even pressed the button to pull the drapes.

I couldn't risk the possibility that somebody else might overhear what I had to say.

"I'm not a *Down with Love* girl, either," I confessed.

Vikki gasped and shook her head.

But I nodded. "I'm a woman who has fallen in love. And I'm going to tell him. Tonight's the night."

CATCHER

"Tonight?!" Peter exclaimed.

"Yep! Tonight's the night Barbara Novak's going down!" I announced. The typewriter was tap-dancing under my fingers. "I've got her just where I want her. She was saying yes, but any man could tell she meant no."

"Uh-oh!" Peter said.

"Here's the title for next month's cover story," I said. I sat back and read from my typed page. " 'Catcher Block on Barbara Novak: Penetrating the Myth.' "

"We'll have to sell it in a brown wrapper," Peter said.

"I'm taking her to my place, which she still thinks is your place, by saying that the guy she thinks I am who acts like you has a meeting there with you and the guy who she doesn't know I really am."

Peter looked confused. "What do I have to say?"

"You don't say a word," I said emphatically.

"Gotcha. So this is it!" Peter said. "Tonight's the night. I have to have my big night with Vikki at the exact same time that you're having your big night with Novak that will ruin Novak and Vikki and everything Vikki's ever worked for! You're putting me under an enormous amount of pressure, Catch! It's enough to make a man explode!"

"Finally." I raised my pencil cup and made a toast. "Here's to tonight!"

Barbara

I t was a two-hour bubble bath night. As I soaked in my tub, gazing at the Manhattan skyline through the French doors, listening to Judy Garland sing "Fly me to the moon and let me play among the stars . . ." I truly felt as if I could.

At last I dragged myself out of the tub and slipped into my favorite Dior corselette. As I sat down at my dressing table, I scanned my collection of perfumes. Tonight, only one would do. My Sin. I dabbed it behind my ears, along my neck, down my cleavage . . .

When Zip finally arrived, I was ready to go out on the town.

But he had one stop he had to make on the way.

"I hope you don't mind this detour," Zip said as we stopped off at Catcher Block's apartment. Apparently he'd set up an appointment for an interview.

"I only mind if Peter MacMannus is wasting your time."

When we reached the apartment, Zip found a note taped to the door.

He peeled it off, opened the note, and read: " 'Dear Zip,

146

Something came up. Accept my apologies with the champagne inside.'"

"Typical," I said with a scowl.

"We might as well at least crack the champagne," Zip said. "We'll just stay ten minutes."

"Ten minutes?"

"Ten minutes," he said confidently.

He slipped the key in the lock and went inside.

Barbara

At the exact same moment that I was heading into Catcher Block's apartment, nearly bursting to tell him my secret, Vikki was having her all-important date with Peter MacMannus.

First, let me explain that I am writing about what happened from a primary source—Vikki's personal diary. Because of the way everything turned out in the end, she agreed to let me have access to it (I mean, she'd already told me almost everything that was in it in vivid detail anyway!) because she thought it was important to the story I'm trying to tell.

Of course, I had to tidy up a few of the more personal thoughts in order to stay off the banned-books list. But except for those small edits, the events are reported exactly.

Here's what happened.

Peter was more than delighted when Vikki insisted they meet for dinner. He took her to a very romantic Japanese restaurant.

Well, Vikki was bubbling over with excitement, all set to

pop the question, but not long after they were seated on the floor cushions at their tiny table, she noticed that Peter wasn't himself. He wasn't talking, for one thing. And he had twisted his dinner napkin into an origami toad.

"Peter," Vikki said gently, "is something wrong? You seem nervous."

"I don't seem guilty!" Peter exclaimed. "What would I have to seem guilty about?"

Vikki was taken aback. "I didn't say 'guilty.' I said 'nervous.'"

"Are you accusing me of keeping something from you?!" Peter squeaked, his voice rising an octave.

People at nearby tables were beginning to stare.

"Peter, calm down," Vikki whispered.

Well, Vikki is one smart cookie, and by that point, she says in her diary, she knew she finally had to face facts about Peter and their relationship.

"It's all right, Peter," she said kindly. "You're not keeping anything from me." She took a deep breath, then whispered confidentially, "I already know."

Peter turned pale. "What?!"

"I know all about it. I've known all along."

"You *have*?!"

"Yes," Vikki replied. "And so what? So you're a homosexual—hopelessly in love with Catcher Block." She shrugged. "That's no reason the two of us can't get married."

"WHAT?!"

At that point, according to Vikki, Peter looked as if he were about to suffer a fatal stroke.

"I'm *NOT—!*" He looked around the restaurant, then lowered his voice. *"I am not a homosexual!"*

"Oh, Peter, come on!" Vikki said, tired of pretending. "The cooking for Catch at his place, the pictures of Catch's parents at your place . . . Believe me, if there had been any other explanation, I would have found it." She chuckled. "At one point I even convinced myself that life was all one big zany sex comedy, and that you had switched keys with the lead to use his swinging pad to snare me!" She laughed ruefully and took a slug of her sake.

Peter grabbed Vikki's hands, nodding like a madman, and whimpered, "I *did*! I *did* switch keys with the lead!"

Vikki rolled her eyes. "Oh, please! If that's not what you feel guilty about, what is?"

"That Catcher Block has been privately tricking Barbara Novak so he can publicly destroy her with one of his exposés!" he blurted out.

"What?!"

Vikki wrote later in her diary that she was very shocked—and outraged on my behalf. (Thanks, Vikki!)

"And you've known about this all along?!" she demanded, like a prosecutor in her final cross-examination.

Peter flinched—then nodded miserably.

Okay, here's where I had to flat-out censor some of

Vikki's language. Suffice it to say that my calm, level-headed editor blew her top.

"Where are they?!" she demanded.

"His place—uh, *my* place! . . . His place," he finally admitted.

Vikki scrambled up from her seat on the floor as gracefully as any woman in a tight skirt, girdle, and six-inch heels could. She glared down at the man she thought she loved. "Good-bye, Peter!" she said resolutely. "The wedding is off!"

Then she retrieved her wrap and ran out to catch a cab.

Peter stumbled to his feet—hopping a little, because his left leg was asleep—then called out, "Where's my geisha? I need my shoes!"

CATCHER

*L*et me see if I've got this," I drawled. "The first button lowers the lights and the second one starts the hi-fi. Shall we go for broke?"

"I'm game if you are, Zip," Barbara said.

"Okay, here we go," I said. We were sitting on the couch in my apartment, sipping champagne. "I think the first button lowers the lights and the second one starts the hi-fi."

Bingo. The lights were low and the music was nice and easy.

Then I touched a third button, on the end-table console, and the couch slowly lengthened to bed size. We laughed, lifting our feet, then relaxed, lying side by side.

Barbara and I turned and faced each other. I took off my Zip glasses and stared into her eyes.

Tenderly I brought my finger to her cheek. Just above a whisper I said, "You have an eyelash . . ." and dabbed her cheek. I lifted the lash and held it to her lips, and said, "Make a wish."

Still looking into my eyes, she made her wish and blew the lash away and smiled.

"What?" I said.

"Funny . . . The way you said 'lash' . . . It sounded like you had a different accent."

Quickly I put the glasses back on. "That is funny," I drawled, being careful to stay in character. "Anyway, guess this sofa bed makes it three out of three! This is definitely a woman-snaring bachelor pad, fully loaded to get you in the mood."

"Are *you* in the mood, Zip?" Barbara asked me.

"Yes, Barbara, I am," I told her earnestly, and put my arms around her. The music on the hi-fi seemed to swell. We kissed passionately until Barbara, needing air, threw her head back. I bit her neck and nibbled on her ear and she writhed in ecstasy.

"Darling, don't! No!" she cried.

"'No'?" I said. "All this time you've waited, and now you're saying no?"

"Yes!" she said breathlessly. "There's something I want to tell you . . ."

I changed position, kissing her eyelids, and pushed a button at the end of the side table. Secretly, soundlessly, above the hi-fi, a reel-to-reel tape machine started to record our every word.

"Yes, Barbara Novak? Tell me everything," I said loudly and clearly for the hidden microphone.

Between deep breaths, Barbara said, "I . . . love . . . you . . ."

"Tell me how much, Barbara Novak . . ." I said, then blew in her ear, driving her wild.

"Too much . . . too much . . . too much to have sex with you!"

I kissed her. "Oh, right . . ." I said, kissing her again, "because you're Barbara Novak . . ." and again, "the author of *Down with Love* . . ." and again, "and you don't believe in having sex with feelings . . ."

"No. That's not why I want you to stop. I want you to stop because I love you too much to have sex without marrying you," she purred. "I want what every woman wants—love and marriage. I'm not a *Down with Love* girl. I'm not the girl you think I am."

"Oh, you're exactly the girl I think you are," I said. "Keep talking, baby. Tell me how you don't really care about being part of the workforce."

With one eye on the tape recorder, I kissed her below the neck, above her breasts. She whimpered in delight . . .

I was on top of Barbara on the couch when I heard a vague noise like a key jiggling in a lock. And then the door swung open and Gwendolyn stepped in.

"Catcher Block!" she shouted.

I lurched forward and my elbow bumped a button. The hi-fi needle whipped hard across the record with a loud zipping noise and all the lights flared on bright.

I rolled off Barbara immediately, but, due to the nature

of what Gwendolyn had interrupted, was temporarily unable to stand and greet her . . . properly.

"You're getting sloppy," she said. "Leaving a key on the outside when you're busy on the inside."

I glanced at Barbara. Her back was turned, but she was examining me closely over her shoulder.

"Why the long faces?" Gwendolyn said. "We're all equal self-reliant citizens of the world here. I know I am. And heaven knows all men are." She looked at Barbara. "And you're with Catcher Block, so I certainly hope you are! Anyway, I just popped by for a little sex à la carte. But since you're busy, I'll just ring up my crew captain at the hotel. Cheerio!"

And she was gone.

Barbara stood there, frozen.

Slowly I pulled off my Zip glasses. I was an experienced enough gambler to know when to cash in my chips.

"All right. Now you know. I'm Catcher Block, not Zip Martin. There is no Zip Martin."

Not a tear, not a shout. She just stood there with her back to me, doing a slow burn, I figured. Well, maybe I had deceived her. But hadn't she done the same thing—to millions? Hadn't she deceived half the planet—the female half—into swallowing her *Down with Love* philosophy? "Before you storm out of here, admit it," I insisted. "Admit I got you. Admit I got Barbara *'Down with Love'* Novak to fall in love."

She didn't admit it. Instead, she walked right by me to the hi-fi and switched off my tape recorder. I was dumbfounded. Then she turned back to me with a look of love.

"I'm not going to storm out of here, Catch. And I'm not going to admit that you got Barbara Novak to fall in love. Because I'm not Barbara Novak. There is no Barbara Novak," said whoever the hell she was.

Barbara

here is no Barbara Novak."

Catch looked as if he couldn't breathe.

How about you, dear reader? Are you surprised?

I know what you must be thinking. Catcher Block has been spilling his guts throughout this book. How did I manage to keep my deepest secrets even from you?

Simple. I'm a better writer. (Sorry, Catch.)

Anyway, if you find this announcement shocking, just wait. There's more.

Lots more.

I knew Catcher Block wasn't Zip Martin from that very first moment I met him in the dry cleaners.

Do you know how I knew?

Because I used to work for Catcher Block.

Uh-huh. That's right. I was his secretary. Secretary number 816, if I remember correctly.

And now it was time to reveal the entire plot.

"And I didn't fall in love with Zip Martin. I fell in love with Catcher Block. And that happened a year ago, when for three and a half weeks I worked as your secretary. I don't expect you to remember me. I wasn't a blonde back then. Although you did ask me out, and it broke my heart to say no. But I loved you too much. I couldn't bear to become just another notch in your bedpost. With your dating habits, I knew even if I was lucky enough to get a regular spot on your rotating schedule, I would never have your undivided attention long enough for you to fall in love with me. I knew I had to do something to set myself apart. I knew I had to quit my job as your secretary and write an international bestseller controversial enough to get the attention of a New York publisher as well as *KNOW Magazine*, but insignificant enough that, as long as I went unseen, *KNOW Magazine*'s star journalist would refuse to do a cover story about it. I knew that every time we were supposed to meet, you would get distracted by one of your many girlfriends and stand me up and that this would give me a reason to fight with you over the phone and declare that I wouldn't meet with you if I lived to be a hundred. Then all I would have to do was be patient for the two or three weeks it would take until everyone in the world bought a copy of my bestseller and I would begin to get the publicity I would need for you to, one: see what I look like, and two: see me denounce you in public as the worst kind of man."

For once, Catch wasn't interrupting. I believe my revelation had deprived him of the ability to speak.

"I knew this would make you want to get even by writing one of your exposés, and to do that you would have to go undercover, assume a false identity, pretend to be the kind of man who would make the girl I was pretending to be fall in love, and I knew that since I was pretending to be a girl who would have sex on the first date, you would have to pretend to be a man who wouldn't have sex for many dates, and in doing so we would go out on a lot of dates to all the best places and all the hit shows until finally, one night, you would bring me back to your place, which you were pretending was someone else's, so that you could get the evidence you needed to write your exposé by seducing me until I said, 'I love you.' But saying 'I love you' tonight was also *my* plan. I just wanted to tell you the truth first, so that when you heard me say '*I* love *you*' *you* would know *I* knew who *you* were and *you* would know who *I* was. Then you, the great Catcher Block, would realize you'd been beaten at your own game by me, Nancy Brown, your former secretary, and once and for all I would have set myself apart from all the other girls you've known, all those other girls you never really cared about, by making myself someone like the one person you truly love and admire above all others—you. And once you realized you had finally met your match, I would at last have gained the respect that would make you want to marry me first . . . and seduce me later."

At last I stopped, spent. I had kept my secret from everyone in the world. Even my editor, Vikki Hiller, had no idea.

It was a relief to reveal myself at last.

I waited, breathless, for Catch's response.

He just stood there a moment while he absorbed everything I'd said. Then he snapped his fingers. "I knew you were a brunette!"

I rolled my eyes. "I knew you'd say that. But I wanted you to hear all this from me before you heard it from your private eye."

The phone rang.

Neither of us moved.

Then, without taking his eyes off me, he answered it. "Yeah."

I didn't have to hear the other half of the conversation. I could look at Catch's face and know who it was and what he was saying.

It was the private eye Catch had hired. And he was saying something like:

"Block? McNulty. Got everything there is on Novak, and it's nothing. Novak doesn't exist, except for a P.O. Box in Maine in care of one Nancy Brown of 28 Gramercy Park, where she was born and raised."

I knew that his desk was probably covered with news clippings and photographs of me as mousy brown-haired Nancy Brown: my high-school yearbook, the clippings, my tap recital, my coming-out dance, a college graduation portrait.

Catch shook his head and I knew the private eye was saying something like:

"And while our Nancy may have broken a few hearts growing up, I can't find the guy we're looking for who broke hers."

"Never mind," I heard Catch say. "I found him."

He hung up the phone. The unflappable Catcher Block was floored. Outfoxed. Outplotted. Outmanipulated. Out of cigarettes. He crumpled an empty package and threw it across the floor.

So you see, dear reader, as Barbara Novak, I had a fake name. A fake bio. Even a fake hair color.

"So now you know everything," I said. And then I took a deep breath and moved to the next, and perhaps final, step in my yearlong plan. "Now tell me the one thing I don't know. Tell me if this plan of mine has worked. Tell me if it's made you fall in love with me as I love you."

In the silence that followed I heard a clock tick away the seconds at excruciatingly slow speed.

I heard a faucet dripping in the kitchenette.

I heard a faint *ding!* Someone getting off the elevator down the hall.

And then I heard music—lush, romantic, drive-in movie music—and to this day I don't know if it was coming from his bachelor-pad stereo or simply playing in my head.

And then we were moving toward each other in slow motion, like that couple in the shampoo ad, until I was in his arms and he was kissing me.

No Zip or Barbara in sight.

Just Catcher Block kissing me, plain old Nancy Brown.

And then I knew at that moment, it had all been worth it. My dreams had come true.

Suddenly Catch opened his eyes and looked around his apartment—and his eyes bulged.

"Come on. We're going out."

"Out?" I said, laughing. "Now? Why?"

"Because," he said firmly, "no wife of mine belongs in an apartment like this!"

Wife? Did he say "wife"? I gazed up into his eyes, melting against him. "Wife?"

"You will marry me," he informed me. Then his voice softened. ". . . won't you, Barbara?"

"Nancy."

He grinned. "Nancy."

"Oh, Catch!" I said breathlessly. "It's all I've ever wanted."

His lips met mine and we lost ourselves in the kiss, until we fell back on the couch, still entwined. Catch moved on top of me. Then I rolled over on him. Then he rolled me back over. Then giggling, I flipped him like a championship wrestler and pinned him to the couch beneath me.

"You don't mind me being on top, do you?" I said, giggling.

"Of course not," he said. "But you could at least wait until I put you there."

We both laughed. I tickled him till he squirmed and cried uncle. "But I don't need you to put me on top," I said, still laughing. "I've gotten there all by myself."

Playfully I hit the buttons on his control pad. The lights went down.

Catch froze. Then he hit the button and brought the lights back on as he mancuvered himself out from under me.

"Very funny, Nancy," he said seriously, straightening his clothes. "But you can stop pretending you're Barbara Novak."

I couldn't help but giggle. Catcher Block, acting like a spinster librarian!

Suddenly the front door banged open, and Gwendolyn the stewardess rushed back into the apartment.

But she hadn't run back to express her adoration of Catcher Block.

She was there to see me!

"You *are* Barbara Novak!" she squealed, grabbing my hands. "I didn't realize! You're my heroine! Well, of course you are, you're the heroine of all women around the world—but you saved my life. Oh, I'm still flying friendly in the skies, but now I decide *how* friendly, and *when*, and with *whom*! Oh! And I'm also training for my pilot's license. And I have you to thank for it. Thank you, Barbara Novak. Thank you for all womanhood!"

She kissed me on both cheeks, then waved and ran back out.

I just stood there, letting her words sink in.

Catch turned to me and laughed. "Wow. Wait until all the women in the world find out the truth. That everything you've done was just a ruse to get me—'just a man.'" He was nearly bent over laughing. "Man! This could be more than a Pulitzer. This could be a Nobel Peace Prize!"

At last his words sank in over Gwendolyn's.

I looked at the man I loved in disbelief. "Catch . . . Darling . . . You're not still going to write your exposé?"

He shrugged, completely clueless. "Why not?"

"You know why not," I said. "For 'all the women in the world.' They look to me—"

"The exposé can't hurt you now," Catch said, wrapping his arms around me. "You're going to have everything you've ever wished for! You'll be Mrs. Catcher Block, living in our dream house in the suburbs, with a yard full of noisy kids . . ."

He gave me a chaste peck on the cheek. "Of course, I'll still have to have my apartment in the city—"

"Catch . . . stop."

Catch stopped and waited expectantly.

In the silence that followed I again heard a clock tick away the seconds at excruciatingly slow speed.

The faucet was still dripping in the kitchenette.

Ding! The elevator again. Maybe Gwendolyn going down.

I sighed. There was really no other way to put it.

"I can't do this."

Before he could respond, the door banged open. Vikki stormed into the apartment. "Barbara! Stop! Don't do this! He's not who he says he is!"

I smiled sadly at the man I loved. The man who wanted to marry me. How could he marry me? He had no idea who I was.

How could he? I was just figuring it out myself. "Neither am I. Good-bye, Catch."

This time I left quickly.

Oh, Catch chased me out into the hall. Followed by Vikki. And just as I stepped onto a down elevator, a bell rang and Peter stepped off of the next one, looking for Vikki.

It was a comedy of errors, and the biggest one was mine.

Barbara

Vikki tried to leave right behind me. But Peter kept blocking her way.

Here's what she wrote in her diary (paraphrased) about what happened.

"Vikki, please, let me explain!" Peter begged.

"There is no explanation," Vikki said, still punching the elevator buttons. Up, down—she didn't care which direction as long as it was away. Away from Peter Mac-Mannus.

"Deceiving the girl you're supposed to marry about your homosexuality is one thing," Vikki said hotly. "Deceiving me in business is another! And I thought you were different! But you're not. You're a rat, Peter Mac-Mannus! You're just like every other man!"

And then she hauled off and slapped him across the cheek—*smack*—so hard, it spun him around, until he found himself face-to-face with himself in the gilded hall mirror.

And suddenly—

He was grinning at his face in the mirror, like a man in a shaving commercial who had just left some babe in bed. "I'm just like every other man!"

Then he spun around, his eyes gleaming as he stared at Vikki.

Something about that look froze her to the spot. She wrote in her diary that the temperature in the hallway seemed to rise at least ten or fifteen degrees. And that before she could move or utter a sound, Peter strode toward her, took her firmly by the shoulders, dragged her against his chest, and kissed her hard, with all the passion of a red-blooded American male in love.

When they finally broke apart, Vikki had turned scarlet, and reported feeling weak-kneed, faint, and quite giddy. And she'd resolved in her mind to her complete satisfaction the issue of this man's homosexuality.

"Peter MacMannus!" she gasped.

With a newfound sense of his masculine power, Peter took the woman he loved by both hands and drew her toward Catcher Block's gadget-filled apartment. "What do you say we step inside?" he said, enticing her with his most seductive smile.

"I . . . I can't . . ." Vikki mumbled, blushing even more as she remembered the switches, the foldout bed . . . "I have to go to . . ." *Uh, what was her friend's name again?* ". . . to Barbara . . ."

"Just for ten minutes," Peter implored.

Vikki couldn't control her foolish grin. "Ten minutes?"

Peter nodded confidently. "Ten minutes."

Vikki was helpless to do anything but allow herself to be tugged through the door.

On the Set of <u>Down with Love:</u> The Movie as Featured in <u>NOW</u> Magazine

Making Down with Love

Most people have to face death to see their lives flash before them.

All I have to do is buy a movie ticket.

Believe me, this way is *so* much more fun!

When I first sat down to type the opening lines of my book, *Down with Love,* I had no way of knowing if my words would ever see the light of day. But thanks to the hard work and creative genius of Vikki Hiller—my fantastic editor (and now dearest friend)—my book was not only published, it became a huge international bestseller.

That alone would have been enough excitement to last a girl two lifetimes. But Vikki never was one to fill the coffee cups halfway. And now, thanks to this gutsy lady, the story of how it all came about has been made into a major motion picture!

Screenwriters Eve Ahlert and Dennie Drake and director Peyton Reed, along with producers Bruce Cohen and Dan Jinks, have done an unbelievable job of breathing movie magic into my story. And I'm absolutely *thrilled* (and terribly flattered!) that casting director Francine Maisler chose the talented and very beautiful Renée Zellweger to play me!

Who could have dreamed up a more perfect cast! Ewan McGregor and David Hyde Pierce are absolutely yummy as best buddies Catcher "Catch" Block and Peter MacMannus. Sarah Paulson is so much like Vikki it's reminiscent of something right out of *The Twilight Zone.* And as for Tony Randall's portrayal of publishing magnate Theodore Banner—well, he can boss me around any day!

During filming, I was delighted to be invited on to the set as a story consultant, where I got to meet the fabulous cast and crew. I've never seen hard work look like so much fun! They even insisted on pulling me on to the set one day as an extra. (Hint: Look for me at the beatnik party!) All I can say is that the movie these talented people have created is as close to my real life as a home movie—only with sound and in Technicolor! Thanks, everybody!

Now, as a special treat for *NOW* readers, we bring you a behind-the-scenes sneak peak at the making of *Down with Love: The Movie*. It's my special way of saying thank you to all my fans who have helped make *DWL* such a cultural phenomenon.

To you, dear friends, I say, remember, Your life is a movie and *you* are the leading lady! Whatever you do, have a ball—and don't give up until you get your hands on that Oscar!

See you at the movies!
Love and kisses (chocolate ones, of course!),

Barbara Novak

The adorable and always chic Renée Zellweger as Barbara Novak.

Handsome Ewan McGregor looks cool with barely a hair out of place—even in his topless silver sports car—as he greets one of the many friendly employees at the Hollywood Center Studio.

ALL MESSENGERS & FOOD DELIVERIES MUST PARK ON THE STREET. NO EXCEPTIONS

Renée looks as if she can just imagine the wonderful scene that director Peyton Reed has just described to her. She'll certainly keep the *bored* out of her next board meeting in this embroidered pink wool jacket over a formfitting sheath dress. The turned-up brim hat and elbow-length gloves in Wite-Out® white complete this smashing but casual office look.

David Hyde Pierce, sporting a heart-stopping red vest, gets the royal treatment in a star-spangled trailer before shooting his next scene. But who needs help when you're that good-looking?

ike a ravenous girl in a
pastry shop, Renée can't
believe all the fashion confections
that have been whipped up just
for her. She keeps her cool in a
bright yellow backless linen dress,
preserving its elegance by adding
a black patent straw Patricia
Underwood hat and midforearm
black gloves.

Cast and crew—a movie is always an ensemble production. Renée gets more than enough help slipping into this matching jumbo houndstooth coat for a gorgeous look that makes it easy on the eyes for her *Down with Love* cameramen.

Who's in charge of *this* scene, hmm? Sarah Paulson shares a lighthearted moment with director Peyton Reed as they work on a scene on the Mahogany Club set. Her shoulder-baring black-and-white-checked dress demands attention at any business lunch.

Sarah shares a kiss over "lunch" with an adoring backstage fan. Love her "fetching" Patricia Underwood black straw hat!

Nice work if you can get it! It's hard to tell who's having more fun in this scene—Ewan or his lovely dancers! If this is how they dress on the moon, then Ewan says, "Save me a seat next to John Glenn!" (Wonder if they can pick up *Bonanza* on those adorable hats!) Ewan looks out of this world in this café au lait suit.

This fantastic duo could cream Batman and Robin any day. But for some reason, Ewan and David insisted on shooting this scene at the Astronette Club over and over again. Tell the truth, boys: Is it because you're such perfectionists? Or did you just want another look at how girls are going to twist and shake in outer space?

Sarah and Renée look like a gift from the fashion gods as their characters arrive at a rooftop supper club for a dinner meeting with Peter MacMannus and Catcher Block. Renée is stunning in a floor-length black embroidered gown worn beneath a stunning one-of-a-kind pink satin evening wrap. Sarah proves that not only are diamonds a girl's best friend, they practically sanctify her when worn with a strapless black matte jersey evening gown topped off with a royal plum silk wrap.

've Got a Secret," Sarah seems to say, "for your lips only!" David's not telling, but his expression is. And no doubt it's all about love.

Renée takes off her gloves in the battle of the sexes, and it looks like costar Ewan is down for the count. But that's okay— they both win in this love match. Renée is a knockout in a white crepe gown with pearl-encrusted bodice. Ewan is wedding-cake perfect in his tailor-made black tuxedo.

Fed Up with Men?
Get...
DOWN WITH LOVE

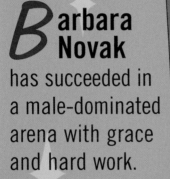

Barbara **Novak** has succeeded in a male-dominated arena with grace and hard work.

Read her inspiring story and take the first step in your quest for success by saying no to love and yes to career, self-fulfillment, and independence!

NOW IN HARDCOVER WHEREVER BOOKS ARE SOLD

Barbara

I thought I'd escaped this time. But I should have known Catcher would follow me out into the night. We were getting to be regulars with our arguments out on the streets of Manhattan. Maybe we should sell tickets!

Except this was the last time I would ever see Catcher Block.

"Nancy, wait! What do you mean, you 'can't do this'?"

I turned around. Might as well get this over with. Set the man straight. Then we could both get on with our lives.

"I mean," I said calmly, "I can't marry you."

"What?!"

"I can't be Mrs. Catcher Block," I said. "I can't be your wife with the kids and the house in the suburbs."

He looked so helpless and confused. I tried to explain, even though I was still in the middle of explaining my confused feelings to myself. "There was one part of my plan I didn't count on. That by pretending to be Barbara Novak, I would actually *become* Barbara Novak. I may be the last woman in the world to do it, but I have finally become a *Down with Love* girl Level Three."

I shook my head with a newfound resolve. "I don't want love. And I don't want you."

A taxi pulled up at the curb, and without another word, I stepped inside.

"What, are you *nuts*?" Catch exploded as he followed me to the cab. "There isn't a woman in your whole upside-*Down-with-Love* world that would say no to a marriage proposal from Catcher Block!"

I almost laughed. Catcher Block would never change— I could see that now. Arrogant and conceited and selfish to the end.

"I guess I've set myself apart again" was all I could say. A bittersweet good-bye.

I closed the door, and the cab drove off as it began to rain.

As we took a right at the corner, I wondered if Catch was still standing there, watching me go.

But this time I didn't look back.

CATCHER

I t was perfect weather for a funeral.

When the doorbell rang, I opened the door to Peter in robe and pajamas. I hadn't shaved.

"What did Vikki say?" I asked hopefully. "Any luck?"

"Nope. Barbara still doesn't want to see you. She's thrown away everything you've sent her—the flowers, the candy, the six-thousand-dollar state-of-the-art Celestron telescope that wasn't really for *you* to send because it was *mine*, not *yours*."

I slumped to the couch. "She hates me."

Peter pouted. "At least Novak dropped you flat. *You* know where you stand." He went to the bar and poured himself a drink. "Sometimes I think Vikki only started talking marriage to me that night to get me to have sex with her. And since I did, I hardly ever see her . . . except when she comes back for more . . . and I always give in . . . Makes me feel so used!" He tossed back the drink, then slammed down the glass.

"It's just not right!" he exclaimed. "I shouldn't feel used. *She* should! But she's taking her cues from Novak! That's why you have to get to Novak! You have to solve this, Catch! You have to squash her! Crush her! If not for the sake of civilization, then just for me!"

"But I don't want to crush her," Catch said. "I love her."

"Fine, all right, so run with that, then. What happened to your idea of making your exposé a public love letter?"

"That's no good. She's *down* with love—for real this time."

"You have to think of something," Peter insisted. "But it's no wonder you can't think in here, it's too stuffy. Come on, get dressed. We're going out. Everyone misses you. Everyone's asking for you—ladies, men, everyone about town. You have to start circulating again. Where's your little black book?"

"I threw it away."

"Man! You've got it bad, and that is not good. You've got to stop holing yourself up in here like some untidy hermit. A man has needs—I know that now—and you need that little black book!"

"Not anymore."

At that moment Yvette came out of the bedroom, all tucked into her uniform, her nose in a little black book. "Thanks, Catch," she said. "That was . . . great," she said, sounding like she was just being polite. "Maybe I'll call you Wednesday and we'll take in a matinee . . ." She called out to the kitchen, "If that's okay with you, Elke."

Peter whipped around and stared as Elke, in her uniform, came out from the kitchen looking in *her* little black book.

"Fine with me," Elke said as if it didn't really matter. "I'm not back until Friday, and I'm seeing the Philharmonic—although I don't know how many of them!"

The girls shared a macho laugh and headed out the door.

Peter shook his head in disbelief. "And all this time I've been feeling sorry for you! Thinking you were miserable living like some sex-starved monk!"

I exploded. "I *am* miserable! I'm having sex, but I'm not enjoying it! I don't care about sex anymore—I just want to be married!"

"Me, too!" Peter said. "But fat chance! Vikki gets one of those little black books, she won't even come to me for sex! These *Down with Love* girls!" He shook his finger toward heaven. "It's revenge! Against men!" Then he shook his finger at Catch. "And it's all your fault, lover boy! That's why they all act like you!"

Peter slammed out.

I sat there a moment. Then I started to smile.

I was onto something.

I dashed to his typewriter, inserted a clean sheet of paper, rubbed my hands together, and started to type.

Barbara

I was sitting under the hair dryer at the beauty salon a week or so later in my olive-and-pink cotton sheath—an outfit that always makes me feel pulled together—trying to keep my mind on the latest issue of *Forbes* magazine when I became aware of a loud conversation between two women over the hum of the dryers.

"Elke, wasn't it wild at Catcher Block's the other night?"

My eyes widened, but I didn't move. I surreptitiously glanced to my left.

One of the women looked vaguely familiar, even though it was a little hard to tell with her hair in curlers, her head stuck in the huge dome of the dryer, and cucumbers on her eyes. Could it be Yvette? The stewardess I'd overheard when I had brunch with Vikki and Peter at the Palm Court all those many weeks ago?

"Yes!" the one named Elke loudly exclaimed. "Crazy!"

I rolled my eyes, steaming a little, whether from the conversation or the dryer, I wasn't a hundred percent sure. *Same old Catch* . . .

174

"I know!" Yvette went on. "It was worse than the week before! Bad enough when he didn't want to go out . . ."

"Now he doesn't even want to stay *in*!" Elke commiserated.

"Jeez!" they both exclaimed at once. "Catcher Block has really changed!"

Ding! A ding of realization rang in my head. Or at least the ding of the hair dryer's timer, signaling that my time was up.

A girl came over and checked my set.

I tucked the bit of news about Mr. Block into my mental research file, for later consideration.

CATCHER

I didn't wait for the elevator. I took the stairs—two at a time—up to *KNOW Magazine*.

I swept through the double glass doors and made a beeline for Peter's office. The reception area and the front offices seemed strangely empty of women. *Probably in the break room*, I thought, *looking at Tupperware*. I had more important things on my mind.

"Stop the presses!" I shouted, bursting into Peter's office. "I've got a cover story here that'll make *KNOW Magazine* sell like *KNOW Magazine* has never sold before!"

Peter just sat there, head in hands.

So he was depressed. What else was new? He'd feel better in a minute.

"Peter!" I shoved the typed pages of my new story into his hands. " 'Catcher Block Exposed: How Falling in Love with Barbara Novak Made Me a New Man.' It's my public love letter. Only it's not from me—at least not the old me—it's from the new me, the new man Barbara Novak could fall in love with!"

Peter still wasn't responding.

"Come on, let's get this to print!" I shouted.

"We're not going to print," Peter lamented.

I had no idea what he was talking about.

Peter huffed in exasperation. "Haven't you noticed—?" He stomped to his office door and threw his hand toward the empty desks.

"The desks," he said. "The *empty* desks."

I still didn't get it.

"We have no secretaries!" Peter shouted. "We had to shut down! Every girl in New York City has left her job. They all want to go to work for your Barbara Novak!"

"Work for Barbara?" I asked, flabbergasted. "Where?"

Peter stormed petulantly across the room to the huge windows behind his desk and pulled the blinds. "Novak topped you again!"

I looked out the window, across the street, and my jaw dropped.

There, one of Manhattan's biggest billboards announced:

THE NEW MAGAZINE FOR THE NEW WOMAN:

Barbara Novak's NOW Magazine:

For Women in the Now

A blowup of the first-issue cover showed me Barbara Novak herself had penned the lead story.

Down with Love

How Nancy Brown Became Barbara Novak

Side-by-side photos showed blond bestselling Barbara Novak next to her true identity—mousy brown-haired secretary Nancy Brown.

Peter was right. Barbara Novak had one-upped me. But it didn't matter.

I had an idea. A fantastic idea. It wouldn't win me another Pulitzer Prize. But I thought it might win me . . . the Novak Prize.

I turned to Peter, my heart pounding. "You want to get married?"

"I thought you'd never ask," Peter said dryly.

"Not to me! To Vikki!"

Peter's face lit up. "Oh! Yes!"

I was already dashing out the door. "Then call her—at noon—and ask her!"

Peter chased after me. "She doesn't let me call her at work. She won't take my call!"

"She'll take this one!" I yelled back over my shoulder.

178

Barbara

Could life get any better?

I was wearing my favorite cape—brown double-faced wool with rolled collar, white patent-leather top stitching, and four oversize white buttons at the neckline—over my favorite figure-hugging sheath—a white silk-and-wool crepe with long sleeves, slightly flared at the wrists, and an asymmetrical wrapped bodice fastened with a large brooch at my left shoulder. A matching white turban and heels pulled the ensemble together in a polished look for the office.

I was head of my own company now, and it was important that I project a smart, refined image.

As I strode down the aisle dividing my office, I smiled and spoke to many of my female employees, who looked happy and busy at their desks. Quite a switch from some of the other offices I've been in.

Was I strutting? Perhaps. But don't you think I'd earned the right to strut a few steps? Unlike most men on top, I well remembered what it felt like to be on the bottom, taken advantage of, treated with little or no respect, or—even worse—casually ignored.

I hoped those memories would make me a better boss.

As I turned the corner to my office, I saw the writing on the wall—in modern gold script—and beamed with pride:

Now Magazine

A Division of Novak/Hiller International

As one of my readers, I hope you share in my moment. For after all, where would I be without all of you who spent your hard-earned dollars (or dollars scrimped over time from your weekly grocery allowance!) to buy a copy of *Down with Love*? My royalties on the copy of the book you bought are *your* share in this success—a venture that I hope over time will touch the lives of millions of women.

With a glow I'd never known before, I strutted the remaining few steps into my executive office.

As I swept off my cape and removed my gloves, I said hello to Vikki, Gladys, and Maurice, who were sitting at the coffee table having a meeting of some sort.

Maurice reached into a carton and proudly held up a new product. A chocolate bar.

But not just your ordinary euphoria-inducing chocolate bar.

A chocolate bar with our very own hot-pink arrow on the wrapper!

"It's here!" Maurice exclaimed. *"Down with Love Chocolate!"* Ecstatic, he read from the label: " 'A mouthful of satisfaction in every bite!' "

"Vikki, you're a genius!" I squealed.

Vikki smiled modestly. "Look, your book got chocolate sales to soar. Why shouldn't we get a piece of the action?"

Gladys licked her chocolate-smeared lips. "They sure kill my craving for sex," she said. "But I find I'm desperate for an almond." She got up and headed for the door. "So maybe the *NOW* bars could have nuts."

Vikki and I laughed as Gladys and Maurice headed out.

I marched over to the giant windows behind my desk and stood looking out at the beautiful view of the city—my city—and the *NOW Magazine* billboard that proclaimed our success.

I had taken my own *Down with Love* advice. I had put love firmly behind me and focused all my attention on my career. And just look what happened! I couldn't have dreamed how well it would all turn out.

Vikki joined me at the window, chuckling. "Boy, am I glad it finally occurred to you that you were a multimillionaire many times over and we could start our own business. To think, I came *that* close to getting married and giving all of this up. I was really starting to believe women weren't cut out for the workplace, when the only problem was the workplace wasn't cut out for women." She glared at the offices across the avenue. "Banner House bastards!"

I understood her anger completely. But I was too happy over our success to dwell on the past. "And word is out that Novak/Hiller International is cut to order. Girls are lined up around the block to interview for the job as my private secretary."

There was a pause. Vikki cleared her throat.

I glanced over, one eyebrow raised in question.

Vikki fidgeted a little, then added delicately, "And that's not all. Catcher Block is here. He wants to see you."

Catcher? Here?

"Well, then, call the guard," I said firmly, "because *I* don't want to see *him*."

I saw her squirm. "You have to see him," she informed me with a shrug. "He's an applicant."

I laughed, certain she was pulling my leg.

But she just shook her head, then jerked her head toward the outer office.

"Oh, for heaven's sake!" I fussed.

"At the risk of sounding like my mother," Vikki said dryly, "just stay perfectly still and let him get it over with." With a rueful smile, she left me to face him alone.

Taking a deep breath, I sat at my polished executive desk and pressed the intercom. "Mrs. Litzer, send in the first applicant, please."

Yes, *that* Mrs. Litzer. The one from the dry cleaners where I first met "Zip Martin." She'd had enough of being bossed around by her old-world husband, and she was a hard worker. I guess, too, she served as a painful but useful reminder of the day I met "Zip Martin" at the cleaners.

"Okay, Novick!" she called out from her very own secretary's desk. "Over and out."

I smiled. I liked Mrs. Litzer's style.

I flicked open my compact and quickly checked my makeup—it's hard to convey managerial authority when your lipstick is smeared—then snapped it shut and waited for my first applicant.

Think Eisenhower, I told myself, straightening my spine.

At last the door opened and Catcher Block stepped in.

Our eyes locked.

He looked good. Good enough to eat. Much better than a *Down with Love* bar. Something melted a little inside me.

But so what? Being a successful woman doesn't mean you don't have feelings. It just means you manage them like anything else in your life.

I steeled myself against his charms and gave him a cold hard stare. "Another ruse, Catcher?" I asked, as if bored by the whole thing. I turned a page of the manuscript on my desk as if preoccupied. Never mind that it was upside down. "You know I have no interest in seeing you."

"But you know you have to." His sly grin annoyed me, but I didn't let it show. "And you know I know you have to. I'm sure you know how things are at *KNOW* ever since your new *NOW*."

I shrugged. "I have no way of knowing how things are now at *KNOW*. I knew how things were at *KNOW* before *NOW*."

"Then you should know now at *KNOW* things are a lot like they are at *NOW*. We have to interview every applicant for every job, and so do you, or you'd be going against *NOW*'s definition of discrimination, and you wouldn't want the readers of *NOW* or *KNOW* to know that, now would you?"

Right about now I was wishing I'd named the magazine something totally different, like *Better Homes and Gardens*, or *Ranger Rick*. But I tried to focus on his point.

Which was—he had me. At least, on the point of the interview. Reluctantly I gave in. But I wasn't going to make it easy for him. "Have a seat, *Mister* Block."

He sat in the chair across the desk from me, crossed his leg—I tried not to admire how not an inch of skin showed between his sock and his cuff—and smiled politely at me. As if we'd never met.

"Your application?" I asked briskly.

He leaned forward and handed me the typed form.

I skimmed the information. "Mmm-hmm, mmm-hmm, mmm-hmm. Oh, dear," I said.

His smug grin slipped a bit.

"Unfortunately, the secretary job doesn't pay quite as well as your current job." I smiled and stood up, announcing the end of our interview. "So that's that. Good-bye,

Mr. Block. Here, have a candy bar for your trouble, and again, thank you for thinking of us." I plucked a *Down with Love* bar from the dish on my desk and handed it to him, along with what I had to admit was his staggeringly impressive résumé.

But Catcher didn't budge. He just lounged back in his chair. "But I'm always thinking of you, Miss Novak. I can't stop thinking of you. And I'd like you to reconsider considering me."

"Even at a pay cut of ninety-six-point-six percent?" I challenged.

He sank even lower in his seat and began to peel the wrapper from his candy bar.

My mouth went dry. A dancer at a strip club on ladies' night—if such a thing had even been invented yet—couldn't have been more seductive.

"It's only money," he said offhandedly. "And besides, I've been on top so long," he drawled, "I thought it might be nice to try a new position."

"And you think you could feel comfortable in a position under a woman?" I challenged him.

"I look forward to it," he said brazenly. "Starting at the bottom . . . working my way up slowly to the top . . ." He took a seductive bite of his candy bar.

Fortunately, Mrs. Litzer kept a pitcher of ice water on my desk at all times—a habit she picked up working in the hot laundry—and I poured myself a sip. I'm surprised it didn't sizzle on my tongue. Or didn't sizzle going down.

"Still"—I managed to keep my voice businesslike—"I'm afraid a man of your . . . 'experience' would be too distracted working in a predominantly female workplace."

"Oh, not at all," Catch insisted. "I'm not really interested in women à la carte anymore. The next time I get involved with a woman, it will be to settle down."

Weakening, I grabbed a candy bar for myself, but my fingers were so shaky, I couldn't tear the wrapper. But this was a chocolate emergency. Rolling back in my chair, I cracked it in half on the edge of my desk, which split the wrapper, then I sank my teeth into the shaft of chocolate and bit off a hunk.

"Well," I said around a mouthful of chocolate, "I wouldn't want you stealing one of the women from my workforce just to put her away in a house in the suburbs."

Catch took another slow bite, then slowly licked the chocolate from his lips. "I wouldn't want that, either," he said. "You see, Miss Novak, I'm what you might call a new man. And I'm looking for a new kind of love."

The chocolate was melting in my hand, so I stuffed the rest into my mouth. "Is that so?" I mumbled with my mouth full.

"You would have read all about it," Catch explained, "the whole world would have read all about it, if you hadn't had to scoop me—and put yourself on top!"

He pulled a sheaf of papers from his inside coat pocket and tossed it on my desk.

I licked the last bit of chocolate from my fingers, then picked it up. What I read shocked me:

CATCHER BLOCK EXPOSED
How Falling in Love with Barbara Novak
Made Me a New Man
by Catcher Block

My temper flared. "Oh, sure," I said. "And to put yourself on top, you just happen to have to expose me as Nancy Brown in your attempt to win the Nobel Prize!"

"I didn't say a word about Nancy Brown," Catch shot back. Then his voice softened. "The only prize I wanted to win . . . was you."

My *Love* bar stuck in my throat—or maybe it was my heart. Either way, I couldn't speak.

Finished with his chocolate, Catch balled up the wrapper and tossed it across the room at the trash. Of course, he easily made the basket.

"That is, until I saw that billboard and realized now you're the one who's only interested in being on top. Crazy, isn't it? That after all our tricking each other, all our game playing, I'm the one who wound up here with a love letter and you're the one who wound up with the scoop."

When I still said nothing, he got to his feet. "I'll keep my eye on the billboards," he said softly. "Maybe someday you'll do a piece on how you became someone in between the mousy little brunette Nancy Brown and the ball-busting blonde Barbara Novak." His eyes bored into mine. "That's a piece I could really go for."

Then he left.

CATCHER

I walked to the elevator counting under my breath, just like the first day I'd met Barbara Novak, just like the first time I'd walked away from her.

One. Same old Catcher, any of the dozen or so girls in the office must have thought, watching me walk away. Same old man's man, ladies' man, and man-about-town.

Two. But I wasn't the same. Not at all.

Three. This time I was praying with each count. Praying that Barbara would call my name.

Four. I remembered she was wearing high heels. How they could really slow a woman down. So I walked slower.

Five. And slower.

Six. Seven.

Nothing.

Eight. Nine. Ten.

I stopped and turned, looking down the corridor at the long rows of secretaries who sat in breathless silence. At Maurice, at Gladys, at Mrs. Litzer and Vikki. At everyone—except the one person I wanted to see.

Heartsick, I turned and jabbed the elevator button.

I heard a sickening *ding!* and the doors whooshed open. And there she was.

There was Barbara, standing inside, grinning at me.

"Sorry, Catch. Scooped you again," she said.

And right before my eyes she reached up and pulled off her turban—and shook out a lush new hairdo of soft red hair.

For once in my life I wasn't sure what to do.

Until she winked at me, and pressed the button that held the doors for me.

I stepped inside and scooped her into my arms, kissed her, and felt my spirits soar. Either that or it was the elevator going up.

"I knew the minute I placed an ad as an equal opportunity employer, you'd be the first to apply for my opening," she said.

We kissed.

"I knew you knew," I said. "That's why I knew you'd let me in to ask you to marry me."

We kissed again.

"But you didn't know I'd say yes," she said.

Another big one.

The elevator stopped and the doors opened on the roof. I carried her over the threshold.

Barbara

A helicopter lowered into view, its whirring blades blowing my hair. But I didn't care. My new looser do required fewer artificial ingredients to look good—just like my new attitude.

A banner on the side of the chopper surprised me: MARYLAND OR BUST.

"Maryland?" I asked, laughing.

"We can get married there on the spot!" Catcher explained. "I'm not letting you get away again. Ever."

"Oh, Catch!" I said.

"I love you, Barbara!"

"I know!" I said.

A rope ladder uncoiled from above.

Still holding me in his arms, Catch stepped onto the ladder, which began to lift us up, up, up, and away into a Technicolor sky.

I'm sure the view was marvelous. But neither Catch nor I noticed.

Barbara

I know you're dying to know what happened with Vikki and Peter, too.

Well, at exactly twelve noon Vikki was dialing the offices of *KNOW Magazine*.

At the same time Peter was calling *NOW*.

Both got a busy signal. But both also got a blinking light on their phone, indicating a call on another line.

Both punched the blinking light.

"I'm sorry, you'll have to hold," Vikki and Peter said at the same time.

"Vikki?"

"Peter?"

"Do you want to marry me or not?" they both said at once.

"I'm not giving up my career!" they both replied.

"I wouldn't ask you to!" both gushed.

"Then it's a deal?" they asked in stereo.

"Deal!" both shouted.

How could they not end up together? They're so much alike.

Barbara

Nine months later . . .

But things didn't end there, dear reader.

Almost nine months to the day after Catch and I got married, we held hands and pressed our noses up against a glass window. I bet you can guess where we were.

Peter and Vikki were there with us, too.

"Beautiful," said a nurse who was standing beside us. "Just beautiful. You must be very proud."

"We are!" Vikki, Peter, Catch, and I exclaimed at once!

You say you're confused?

Oh, I get it. You thought we were pressing our noses against the glass window of a nursery in a hospital, admiring a new baby!

Well, maybe one of these days. But not yet.

We were looking in the window of Scribner's bookstore, the one Vikki and I had gone to so many months ago, where we'd found one copy of my book back near the rest rooms.

But today we'd made the window. That's right—life-size cutouts of Catch and me were propped in the front window, advertising *our* new book:

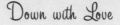

HOORAY FOR LOVE

by Barbara Novak-Block and Catcher Block

a.k.a. Mr. and Mrs. Catcher Block

Published by Novak-Block/Hiller-

MacMannus International

They had even piped in the theme song to *Hooray for Love*—the very version that Ella Fitzgerald sang on *The Ed Sullivan Show* to promote the new book. That song will always be *our* song.

Hip, hip, hooray!!!

Excerpts from Barbara Novak's

Down
with
Love

Introduction

Down with Love. It's a funny title for a book written by a woman.

From the time we're born, our lives as girls seem to revolve around love. We're given baby dolls to love and nurture. Our favorite games are playing house and dressing up like Mommy, the goddess of love. Our first crushes are our daddies, who leave us every day to go off to that mysterious place called work.

Is it any wonder we women are in love with love?

As Lord Byron said, "Man's love is of man's life a thing apart, / 'Tis a woman's whole existence."

So why do I say "Down with love"? Because I think women deserve more.

Let us take one woman, for example. We'll call her Betty Jones.

Even before Betty can roll her hair or shave her legs,

197

she's writing in her diaries about the boy next door—who's a lot more interested in oiling his baseball mitt or building a soapbox car for the next derby than he is in talking to her.

As she grows older, Betty's life revolves around love—and, in particular, whether she is "lovable" enough. The most important thing as she heads to school is not her homework but her hairdo. She spends most of the week worrying about the weekend—hoping she won't be sitting home alone by the phone come Saturday night. She takes home economics to learn how to cook and clean and sew, and typing so she'll be able to eke out a living until she marries and can stay home to cook and clean and sew.

No one ever bothers to ask Betty what she'll be when she grows up because everyone already knows: Betty will be a wife and mother. To love will be her career.

Then one day something special happens to Betty. The man of her dreams—or, at least, a man who's dependable, has a steady job, and has no major disfigurements—finally asks Betty to be his bride. Betty is thrilled! She feels as if she's won a prize! She's Queen for a Day!

But what has Betty really won, my friends?

She is no longer herself, no longer Betty Jones. She has become "Mrs. His Name."

After a lifetime of learning how to act like a lady, she is in for a real eye-opener on her wedding night when she realizes the man she married expects her to behave like a lady everywhere but in the bedroom.

Following the honeymoon, Betty settles into her life as

a wife in the suburbs. Before she knows it, she has a house full of freckle-faced kids—adorable, yes, but one of them always seems to have a cold or the measles or a broken arm. She soon catches on that she is not just a wife, but a cook, maid, nurse, baby-sitter, and taxi driver, that she's on call twenty-four hours a day and rarely gets to leave the "office," and has to squirrel away change from her weekly grocery allowance just to buy bobby pins. She rarely sees the man of her dreams except in her dreams because he's always at the office, commuting to and from the office, or recovering from all his hard work at the office on the golf course or in front of that little black-and-white TV yelling at some referee—when he's not yelling at Betty to keep those kids of hers quiet so he can hear the G.D. game.

Before long, Betty has exhausted her entire repertoire of dinner menus and her husband begins to get bored with her cooking. He calls from the office to say he'll just "grab something" in the city because he's "working late."

Meanwhile, Betty sits at home worrying about what—or whom—he's grabbing.

So Betty's at home in the suburbs up to her elbows in chores, doing all the dirty work, while some other gal is in the city up to her elbows in diamonds, having all the dirty fun—with Betty's husband.

Worst of all, if Betty blames anybody, she blames herself.

Well, I say, "It's a new decade, Betty! That's no longer the way we cookies crumble. You deserve more!"

"But, Barbara," you single women may be saying, "I

don't mind spending every waking hour trying to make myself perfect in order to catch the man I love. It's worth it! I don't mind giving up my opinions, my desires, my hopes and dreams to please him—because all I want is what every woman wants: love and marriage, a home to clean, and children to take to the pediatrician."

And to that I say, "Are you happy?"

"But, Barbara," you married women may be saying, "I love being a cook, maid, nurse, baby-sitter, and taxi driver to my husband and children, because I love them. I don't mind having no time to myself, outside of an occasional bridge game, coffee klatch, or Tupperware party, to do what I want, to pursue my hopes and dreams. Being a cook, maid, nurse, baby-sitter, taxi driver *is* my dream."

And again, to that I say, "Are you happy?"

If you're sitting there feeling sorry for yourself, denying your feelings, or kicking yourself for being a fool, what I want you to know is that you are not alone. You are in good company. To coin a phrase, we have all been there and done that.

Some people may say, "Well, that's life."

But to the Betty Joneses of this world, I say, "The times they are a-changin'."

Hold on to this book, sisters—and maybe sit down. Because it's time we women joined the Jet Age!

Down with Love Principle #1

Women will never be happy until they are self-fulfilled.

I know. It's a shocking, groundbreaking thought. Take

a deep breath, make yourself a teensy little martini if you need it, and then read on.

Down with Love Principle #2

Women will never be self-fulfilled until they attain equality and become independent as individuals by achieving equal participation in the workforce.

Wait! Don't close this book!

You may be shocked. You may be laughing! You may think this book is for some Vassar-educated career gal in glasses who couldn't get a man even if she wanted one. Perhaps you are saying, "But, Barbara, I'm just an ordinary girl. This book isn't for me." But I say, "Yes, dear reader, this book is for you—it's *especially* for you."

This book is for you, the farm wife, with callused hands and premature gray hair, serving a dinner of homegrown vegetables (grown, picked, washed, and cooked by you) to ten noisy freckle-faced children and your stony-faced husband.

It's for you, the wife and mother in an affluent suburb serving her modern family TV dinners before volunteering for the PTA and the church bazaar.

It's for you, the girl working the switchboard and wishing your life was half as exciting as what you're hearing on those party lines.

For you, the secretary (substitute wife), typing, filing, answering phones, and basically running your boss's office for a paltry salary until some man sweeps you off your feet and takes you home to do all his work for free. A girl who maybe, just once, sat in the boss's chair and wondered what it would be like to view the world from the other side of the desk—and, yes, even have someone else make the coffee.

I know you're out there, and I know you know what I'm talking about.

Who am I to be telling you this? What are my credentials for telling you to turn your world upside down?

I am you. I'm a working girl. A girl from Anywhere, U.S.A. A girl who late at night, when the rest of the world is fast asleep, lies awake in bed gazing up at the stars, wondering if there's something more to life than what she's been handed.

I think there's a whole world out there just waiting for us—but we have to go out and get it ourselves. I spent a year writing this little pink book. And I hope it changes your life forever.

Here's the secret, ladies: You've got to do what men do. You've got to put yourself first.

"But, Barbara," you're saying. "I—I don't know how to put myself first. No one ever gave me permission to do that. No one ever taught me how."

Well, I, Barbara Novak, am giving you permission to give *yourself* permission.

And now I'm going to teach you how.

You start by saying, "Down with love!"

Chapter 1

Level One: Down with Love

Love is a distraction. On the road to success, you cannot think about love and keep your mind on your driving. You'll wreck the car. And we all know how costly that damage can be.

So your first step is this: Dump love before it dumps you.

I am completely serious about this. And you have to go all the way. You must completely eliminate love from your life.

"But, Barbara, won't the world fall apart?" you ask. "Won't the human race as we know it die out and disappear from the face of the earth?"

Not at all. Notice I said eliminate *love* from your life. Not *sex*.

Many people believe that it is a scientific fact that for women love and sex are the same thing. But if you follow my complete Down with Love program, you will learn how to differentiate between the feelings of physical lust and emotional love. Men do it all the time. Believe me, as a farm girl from Maine, I know the difference.

By Level Three, you will be able to have sex anytime you like—without love—and enjoy it the way a man does—à la carte. You may even find you'll be able to give up indulging in the *dulces*. (See more about this subject in my chapter seven: "Up with Chocolate.")

Which leads me to:

Down with Love Principle #3

Women should abstain from love, but not sex. You may give a man your body, but not your heart.

"But, Barbara," you may be saying, "I couldn't possibly have sex with a man I wasn't in love with."

But I say that you can and you will. Even more shocking: you might actually enjoy it. Once you are able to get those physical needs met, you will eliminate those vague sensations of longing that we women mistakenly call love.

Only then will you be able to go into the workplace and pay attention to what you're doing.

Ready? Let's begin.

You must follow each step exactly—as specifically as if you were following a quick-weight-loss diet in the *Ladies' Home Journal*. Yes, it may be painful, but only for a short time. Keep in mind that if you skip a step, you may not achieve the results you desire.

WEEK 1

1. Abstain from all men. No exceptions. This is an extreme but necessary first step to cleanse your palate and undo years of bad habits. You must completely eliminate men from your life. This includes the milkman, the mailman, your mechanic at the garage, Uncle Louie, and Cousin George. Even Baby Butch. I don't care if they're eight months old or eighty years old. They're all part of the conspiracy.

2. Turn down all dates. You are not to go out with any man for any reason, especially one that could involve a romantic situation. This includes breakfast, lunch, dinner, coffee, neighborhood block parties, all check-ups with your male gynecologist, or cochairing a Cub Scout fund-raiser.

3. If you are in love with a man, break up with him immediately. If you are married to a man, lock him out of the bedroom and make him sleep on the couch. No matter how much he begs or threatens, you must not give in. Once you have achieved maximum Down with Love control in Level Three, you may be able to resume a relationship with this person.

4. Abstain from all sex. Of ANY kind. This includes coitus, oral sex, full-body massage, heavy petting, hugging, kissing, slow-dancing, and footsie. A sex fast will help eliminate the feeling that the pleasures experienced during the sex act are related to love.

5. Boycott all soap operas. If you must watch TV, hold out for the evening news or a good nature program on animal mating habits (note how the word *love* never comes up).

6. Throw out all your romance novels. Better yet, burn them! That way no other woman can be brainwashed by the outdated romantic story lines. *Gone with the Wind* is acceptable to keep once you have reached Level Three—Scarlett scores pretty high in the putting-herself-first category, but loses points for making such a fool of herself over Ashley.

7. Buy a good sex manual and read it completely. Don't be squeamish. No athlete goes to the Olympics without doing his homework on the sport. For those who are reluctant to ask their local booksellers for adult reading material, see the Appendix for a list of suggested titles and some mail-order companies who will send you their product wrapped in plain brown paper.

8. Do not say, think, or write the word *love* anywhere—not even on a greeting card to your mother. Unless it's to say . . . DOWN WITH LOVE!

FURTHER SELECTED PASSAGES FROM
Down with Love

Barbara Novak on Chocolate

According to Professor Laura M. Gottlemeyer of the University of Vienna, the female has a biological reaction to chocolate that triggers the same pleasurable response in the brain as those triggered during sex. It also improves one's mood by boosting brain levels of the chemical serotonin—much like some antidepressants and other prescription drugs, but without serious side effects. (Well, you do have to watch those calories. But by Level Three, you'll be dropping any unwanted pounds easily through the high-intensity workouts involved in your revitalized sex life.)

This is why chocolate is a key element of the Down with Love program. By substituting chocolate for sex, the woman will soon learn the difference between sex and love. Love for a man will no longer occupy her mind.

Once the woman will no longer be devoting her time and energy to making herself attractive to the chocolate, or making a home for the chocolate, or making herself seem interested when the chocolate tells her how its day went, she will find she has the time and energy to move on to Level Two—where taking on new challenges will lead her to the self-sufficiency of Level Three—where the woman becomes active in the workforce, earning and achieving an unequivocal equality with men.

The ancient Aztecs and Mayans discovered chocolate thousands of years ago. They believed chocolate was a gift from Paradise delivered to mankind by the god Quetzalcoatl, who came to Earth and taught people how to make a drink from the beans of the cacao tree. They believed drinking this dark bitter brew gave one power and knowledge. The Aztec king Montezuma drank chocolate every day to boost his sexual powers, but women were not allowed to drink it. (Naturally.) Lucky for us, when it spread to Europe in the 1600s the rich and elite discovered the pleasure of adding sugar to give it sweetness, and so chocolate truly became a gift from heaven.

During Level One, whenever you feel the urge to merge, you must immediately consume chocolate. Make sure your kitchen is well stocked. I recommend keeping your favorites in every room of your house. Always be prepared and carry chocolate with you in your purse, especially if you're going out for the evening.

Just remind yourself of all the reasons why chocolate is better than sex:

- Good chocolate is easy to find.
- Chocolate satisfies you even when it's gone soft.
- You can make chocolate last as long as you want it.

- You can have chocolate on your desk without upsetting your boss.
- Chocolate doesn't care what you look like.

Barbara Novak on Dating

There are nine men on a baseball team. (I know, I looked it up.) What's that got to do with romance?

It's the number to remember. The Down with Love girl should never be dating fewer than nine men at any one time. That gives you a week's worth of men, plus two for backup, in case any of them gets sick or has to go visit his mother.

With so many men to choose from, it will be impossible to pick just one to fall in love with, since everyone knows women can never make up their minds. (That's a joke.)

In the beginning you will simply go out and have the time of your life. Not a bad prescription, hmm? Dinner, dancing, theater, museums—you can have it all as long as you go out with them all. And if you find yourself favoring any particular man, immediately eliminate him from your little black book and find a replacement.

Once you are at Level Three, you should have sex à la carte as often as possible. Concerned that all this social activity will wear you out for work? Don't be. It will make you more efficient at the office.

Men know this. They know that they can swing every night and still hit the office like Tarzan the next day. Sex is like food. A person who goes hungry can't concentrate on anything else. But a person who is satisfied goes to work free to think about more important things.

Barbara Novak's Down with Love Do's and Don'ts

After an evening of sexual frolics:
DO NOT LINGER. Get up immediately and leave the room. No matter how comfortable and cozy you feel.

DO NOT spend the night.

DO NOT clear a tiny place in the medicine chest for your toiletries.

DO NOT sleep over, do not let him keep you up all night snoring and grabbing the covers. And most important:

DO NOT—I repeat!—DO NOT slip out of bed in the morning before he does to make him coffee and pancakes in the shape of little hearts carved with your combined initials.

DO enjoy your evening.

DO make sure you have cab fare so you can leave on your own terms.

DO go home, remove your makeup, apply the best firming night cream you can afford, and then . . .

DO get a good night's sleep!

I guarantee you will feel wonderful in the morning—and with no morning-after regrets.

The Confessions
of Catcher Block

NOVAK EXPOSÉ/Block
First draft

CATCHER BLOCK ON BARBARA NOVAK:
PENETRATING THE MYTH

by Catcher Block

Barbara Novak.
If you don't know the name by now,
you've either been orbiting this big
blue marble we call Earth or hiding from
the Russians in a bomb shelter for at
least six months.
Barbara Novak.
The name causes unladylike riots among
otherwise mature females, and strikes
terror in the hearts of the world's most
courageous men.
And all it took was one tiny pink book
full of fairy-tale nonsense called Down
with Love.
One can't escape her. Her words
bombard us from every television news
program. Her smile—arrogant and smug—
accosts us from every newsstand we pass.
She's even managed to infiltrate our
family entertainment venues, such as the

unprecedented promotional performance by a top-line songstress on <u>The Ed Sullivan Show</u> (Judy, baby, what were you thinking?!). It's media hype worthy of P. T. Barnum himself. And just as big a circus.

Barbara Novak's international bestseller <u>Down with Love</u> (which undoubtedly earned both her and publisher Banner House a pretty penny) set her up as the last word on equality in the workplace for women. Miss Novak's prescription: sex without love and a steady diet of chocolate. (I'm sure the Swiss are happy.)

But now fans of Miss Novak are apt to say, "Physician, heal thyself."

<u>KNOW Magazine: For Men in the Know</u> wanted to know:

Is Barbara Novak for real?

Does she practice what she preaches?

And more important to our national security, how does one petite librarian from New England wield more undercover world power than JFK, Castro, and Khrushchev combined—with just a few strokes (of her typewriter)?

Hold on to your receipts, folks. You

may be hitting the bookstore for a refund after this exposé.

Working from a hot tip, KNOW Magazine: For Men in the Know sent its top, Pulitzer Prize-winning reporter out to get to the bottom of Miss Novak. And he used every available tool—journalistic and otherwise—to get the inside story.

It seems a certain astronaut named Zip Martin has splashed down in Miss Novak's life, and frankly, the girl is in orbit. Who is Zip Martin? A bookish, pipe-smoking Oklahoman whose idea of a night out is stopping off at the library on the way home from the launchpad. At least, that's who Miss Novak thinks he is.

In fact, Zip Martin is the clever disguise of a certain ladies' man, man's man, and man-about-town named—you guessed it—yours truly, Catcher Block.

Several times over the last few weeks I've attempted to interview Miss Novak for this magazine—to no avail. Our appointments were repeatedly canceled. Was it something I said? We'd never even met.

So you can imagine my surprise when

Miss Novak used a guest appearance on the show _Guess My Game_ to make disparaging remarks about me to a national audience. (Apparently she categorizes me as one of the men she describes in chapter eight: Men Who Change Women As Often As They Change Their Shirts. Although frankly, I've never heard any complaints before about being a well-dressed, or undressed, man.) I knew then that the only way I'd get my interview was to go undercover. Little did I know my tiny deception would lead Miss Novak to a game called love.

I met Miss Novak as Zip Martin ostensibly by chance, in a dry-cleaning establishment under the management of one of her _DWL_ operatives. Miss Novak's attraction to the man she considered an innocent, homespun astronaut was immediate. She practically threw herself at me. If you don't believe me, just ask the lady at the dry cleaners.

Granted, Miss Novak's initial interest in me as Zip Martin was probably sex only. As the _DWL_ girl, she'd been blacklisted by every red-blooded male on the planet, so it was quite obvious that instead of dining nightly à la carte, she had been doing a lot of cooking at home. Alone.

No wonder the poor girl is starved.

Enter Zip Martin: poor, ignorant, aw-shucks astronaut from Oklahoma. Recently returned from a news-deprived trip in outer space around Mother Earth. As good-looking as Catcher Block, only with a drawl.

But Miss Novak's plans to turn the O-boy into her boy toy went most frustratingly awry when she discovered that Zip had some rather annoying standards of decency and moral correctness. Zip was a romantic. He thought love and sex went together, for gosh sakes.

Miss Novak and Zip Martin dated extensively over the next few weeks. But no matter how much Miss Novak insisted on taking their relationship to a deeper level, Zip Martin persisted in resisting. Apparently, it had been a long time since anyone had told Miss Novak no.

The results, to put it mildly, were

that Miss Novak fell for him like a ton of bricks.

Which, if you've actually read the book, is a big <u>Down with Love</u> no-no. The cornerstone of Miss Novak's twisted theory is, to put it politely, that it's okay for a woman to share her every body part, just not her heart.

The conversion of <u>DWL</u>'s own Barbara Novak may only tell us something we've known all along—that the real goal of all women is not equality in the <u>workplace</u>, but marriage and domination in the <u>homeplace</u>. Not to free all gals—excuse me—women, but to leg-shackle all men. And it's not a new book, Miss Novak. It's a story as old as Adam and Eve.

As Zip Martin would say, this may be the first time we're actually reading Barbara Novak loud and clear.

Nevertheless, <u>KNOW Magazine: For Men in the Know</u> would never want to be accused of being unfair.

So why not let Miss Novak speak for herself?

Here, for the first time anywhere, is a transcript of Miss Barbara Novak's exact words on the subject of love, recorded on the top-of-the-line reel-to-reel tape recorder in my very own apartment:

MISS NOVAK: (Gasping) Darling! Don't! No!

ZIP MARTIN (aka this reporter): No?! After all this time you've waited, and now you're saying no?

MISS NOVAK: (Breathlessly) Yes! (Loud kissing sounds.) There's something I want to tell you . . .

ZIP MARTIN: Yes, Barbara Novak? Tell me anything.

MISS NOVAK: (Moaning) I . . . love . . . you.

ZIP MARTIN: Tell me how much, Barbara Novak.

MISS NOVAK: Too much . . . too much to have sex with you!

ZIP MARTIN: Oh, right. Because you're Barbara Novak, the author of <u>Down with Love</u> . . . and you don't believe in having sex with feelings . . .

MISS NOVAK: No. That's not why I want you to stop. I want you to stop because I love you too much to have

sex without marrying you. I want what
every woman wants, love and marriage.
I'm not a <u>Down with Love</u> girl. I'm not
the girl you think I am.

ZIP MARTIN: Oh, you're exactly the girl
I think you are. Keep talking, baby.
Tell me how you really don't want to
be part of the workforce . . .

CATCHER BLOCK EXPOSED:
HOW FALLING IN LOVE WITH BARBARA NOVAK
MADE ME A NEW MAN

by Catcher Block

Ladies' man, man's man, man-about-town—I was all of the above, and it was all I needed.

Until now.

For now it seems a certain author named Barbara Novak has entered my life, and frankly, I'm writing off my old ways.

Who is Barbara Novak?

If you don't know the name by now, you've either been orbiting this big blue marble we call Earth or hiding from the Russians in a bomb shelter for at least six months.

Everyone knows her as the <u>Down with Love</u> defender of a woman's right to equality in the workplace and the love department. That's who they think she is anyway.

In fact, Barbara Novak is the name of the girl I left behind—but never will again.

Several times over the last weeks I made appointments for an interview for KNOW Magazine—then stood Miss Novak up. If I'd only known what I was missing. When other opportunities knocked, I answered, shutting the door on Miss Novak time and time again.

But then I began to get interested in Miss Novak. Especially after I began taking down quotes.

She called me one of those men from chapter eight: "Men Who Change Women As Often As They Change Their Shirts." On national television, no less.

Ouch.

She called me, and I quote, "someone who fills up the space in a magazine between the advertisements."

Double ouch.

With my male ego wounded, and my dating schedule devastated by Down with Love, I went undercover to prove Barbara Novak a fake.

Instead, I found out that I was the fake.

<u>KNOW Magazine</u>: For Men in the Know
sent its top, Pulitzer Prize-winning
reporter out to get to the bottom of
Miss Novak. And he used every available
tool—journalistic and otherwise—to get
the inside story.

Yours truly, Catcher Block, pretended
to be sweet, innocent Zip Martin,
astronaut from Oklahoma, who never heard
of her or her book—and liked her anyway.

As Zip Martin, I tricked her, lied to
her, and manipulated her.

And she liked me anyway.

As Zip Martin, I got to hear her tell
me what she thought of Catcher Block,
and I quote:

"That's how he operates," she once
told me. "He tricks people into doing
things completely out of character, and
the people don't even know they're being
tricked. Makes you wonder if he's ever
written an honest word in his life." And
later she added, "He's nothing more than
an amoral insidious sneak."

That's when I made my real undercover
discovery. My real exposé.

As Zip Martin, I got to step outside
my role as Catcher Block, ladies' man,

man's man, man-about-town, and I saw
somebody I didn't like.

Myself.

Then the author of <u>Down with Love</u>
walked out on me—the real me. Catcher
Block. And I got a taste of my own
medicine.

Hurt and confused, I was going to
write my exposé anyway. Believe me, I
tried. I made a valiant effort to be the
same merciless journalist I'd always
been. But my heart was no longer in it.

Or maybe I couldn't write it because
at last I'd found my heart.

Now I hope that Miss Barbara Novak
won't always be <u>Down with Love</u>.

As Zip Martin might say, I hope you're
reading me loud and clear. Catcher Block
the ladies' man, Catcher Block the man's
man, and Catcher Block the man-about-town
is signing off.

He's fallen in love.

I've been relying on my great big
Pulitzer for far too long. But now I'm
putting a clean sheet of paper in the
typewriter. I'm going to try one more
time to write something honest, straight
from the heart, all gimmicks aside.

And all my years as a writer are
useless to me if my words fail me now.

Dear Barbara,

Will you marry me?
I love you,

                                        Catch